OPEN HOUSE

Also by William Katz

Death Dreams*

Surprise Party

Published by
WARNER BOOKS   *forthcoming

OPEN HOUSE

WILLIAM KATZ

WARNER BOOKS

A Warner Communications Company

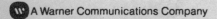

1

"**M**a'am, this is RCA."

"Yes? About my television?"

"That's right, ma'am. Just wanted to confirm the appointment for tonight."

"Eight o'clock?"

"Correct. I'll be over. Remember, it's a safety recall. Please don't let anyone else touch the set."

"Oh, I won't. There's no one else here."

"Good, ma'am. Very good."

The repairman hung up, then left the phone booth. He got back into his red Ford, crossed the Fifty-ninth Street Bridge into Manhattan and drove through Central Park to the West Side.

How perfect it was, he thought. The plan was precise, thoroughly prepared, brilliantly conceived. It would work, just as it had worked before.

He'd memorized Deborah Moore's address on West

Eighty-second Street. He made sure to park two blocks away. He removed his tool kit from the trunk, locked the car and started walking toward Deborah's building. It was a steamy July night, the kind that sent the poor into the streets for fresh air, and kept the affluent inside for machine-conditioned air. The repairman, though, hardly noticed anyone in the streets around him. He walked casually, as anyone would while making an overtime repair call.

Within a few minutes he arrived at Deborah's building, a six-story red brick affair built in 1935. There was no doorman. A visitor had to press an intercom button in the outer vestibule and be admitted by buzzer. The repairman pressed 4J.

Deborah's voice, thin and metallic through the tiny speaker, replied. "This is 4J."

"RCA," the repairman said.

She pressed her buzzer, unlocking the building's front door, and the repairman was inside.

He chose to take the stairs to the fourth floor, avoiding the elevator. He walked down the fourth-floor corridor, where aromas of recently cooked dinners still lingered, and knocked on 4J's green metal door.

Deborah Moore opened. She was of medium height with long, mousy brown hair, and still dressed in the pink cotton dress she'd worn during her day as a researcher in an investment firm. Yes, she would do, he thought.

"Thanks for coming," she said, letting him in. "I'm glad the thing didn't blow up in my face."

"Oh, I doubt it would've blown up, ma'am," the repairman said. "But . . . sparks and fire. I mean, Je-zus, we had a guy out in Islip, you know, Long Island . . ."

"I've been there."

"Well, this guy, we warned him. And he used it and used it. He didn't give a— So it caught fire."

"Was he hurt?"

"He was lucky. He got out. But the whole living room, Je-zus." The repairman looked around. He rubbed his right ear. "Uh, ma'am, if you could . . ."

"Oh, it's over there, inside that cabinet. It's one of those built-ins."

"Yeah. I seen 'em. Hate those things. Y'know, especially with a fire hazard. You should really keep a set out, where air can get to it."

"I'll remember that," Deborah said. She really wasn't very interested. She had a briefcase full of work.

"Let me get to it," the repairman said, moving toward the cabinet and pulling out the TV. Deborah went to open her briefcase.

She looked back at the repairman. Although he was unscrewing the back of the TV, he was staring at *her*. It wasn't an evil stare, not even a suspicious one, but it *was* a stare, as if he were studying her. She was attractive, used to being looked at, but it seemed odd for a man to be working on a high-voltage device and staring at her at the same time.

"Can I get something for you?" she asked.

"Oh . . . no," the repairman replied. He removed the back of the set, then started probing inside.

It took ten or fifteen minutes for him to complete the job. "There we go," he said, "all replaced. You won't have anything to worry about now."

"Good. I'm glad you came," Deborah answered. She was now sitting on her couch reviewing papers. "See anything else wrong in there?"

"Not particularly," the repairman replied. "I always like the old sayin', if it ain't broke, don't fix it. Set works, don't it?"

"Oh yes."

"Color good?"

"Sure."

"Sound?"

"Yes."

"They're makin' em' better all the time. I wouldn't worry. I'd say she'd go, oh, maybe six years heavy use. In the old days, with the tube sets, you'd be poppin' tubes in forever. Y'know?"

"Yes, I remember my father's," Deborah replied. "Oh, what do I owe you?"

"No charge on a safety recall, ma'am."

"That's very good."

The repairman started easing the set back into the cabinet. "Glad this is my last call," he said. "I'm just gonna go get a Coke or somethin', then drift home."

"Oh, let me get you something to drink," Deborah replied, putting her papers beside her.

"Y'know, I'm gonna accept that," the repairman said. "My mouth is a heat wave." Maybe she was the one, he thought.

"Well, the weather has just been so . . . what do you prefer?"

"Oh, Tab. Some diet drink."

"I've got Diet Coke."

"Sure. Great, ma'am. Not too much trouble, is it?"

"Not at all." Deborah walked toward the kitchen.

"One of these days I'll get myself an air conditioner," the repairman said after her.

"You should." Deborah called out as she fidgeted inside her refrigerator for the can. "Working for RCA, you can probably get a pretty hefty discount."

"Yeah. We got the company store. It's okay. So I'll get one and just lie there watchin' the tube."

"Not married?"

There was a pause before the answer. Deborah cracked

open the can, and the repairman could hear the fizz. "No, not married," he replied with a sigh. "Never married. No prospects."

Deborah returned to the living room with two Diet Cokes, a chunk of pound cake and a knife. She set it all down just as the repairman secured the set back in the cabinet. "Please sit down," she told him.

"Oh, thanks," he answered. He sat on a director's chair near a small round glass table. It struck Deborah as odd that he didn't wash his hands. She'd offered drinks to many repairmen, and all had been sure to wash their hands before drinking. Well, what did it matter? The man was thirsty—pushing an appliance truck around New York in the heat, getting screamed at by irate TV owners who'd been without their sets. Let him drink.

The repairman drank a few sips, then leaned back, apparently satisfied by a very small amount of liquid. "It gets lonely sometimes," he said.

"Yes," Deborah agreed.

"You don't . . . ?"

"Live with anyone?"

The repairman shrugged. That's what he meant.

"No. I did, but I don't."

"Yeah. These things fade. You, uh, should have an easy time of it."

Deborah squirmed a little in her chair. She sensed where this conversation was going, and she didn't like it. She detected a change in the repairman's pattern of speech— from the laborer's slang of a few moments before to something more refined, more educated, as if there were two people inhabiting that body. For a moment, she thought he looked familiar. But . . . not really. "Sometimes easy, sometimes hard," she said coldly. "Please drink more." She conspicuously looked at her watch.

"In a rush?"

"I have work."

"Yeah," he said, a touch of disgust in his voice.

She didn't respond. She was starting to feel that something was wrong. Very wrong.

"Look, let me ask you something," he said, getting up, approaching her, towering above her. "One question."

* * *

Ten minutes later a neighbor heard Deborah's vacuum cleaner running. He thought it was odd, for she always cleaned her apartment on the weekend, and, besides, who wanted to run a vacuum cleaner in that heat, with the little air conditioning that the building provided? Maybe she was having guests. Or maybe something had spilled. Nothing to worry about.

Deborah's body was discovered an hour later by a visiting girlfriend who had a key. Deborah lay on her back on the living-room floor, a startled expression on her face, a puncture wound in her chest. Everything around her was neat. The carpet had been vacuumed. Two glasses of Diet Coke still rested on a table. Aside from the body, the scene was thoroughly peaceful.

Leonard Karlov squeezed a printed form with three carbons against Deborah Moore's kitchen wall. He took out a sixty-nine-cent ballpoint pen and started filling in the data required by the New York Police Department. He refused to sit on the couch, or even a kitchen chair. That would have been disrespectful. Besides, some strand from that couch or chair could prove crucial. The wall near the stove was safe, and Karlov would not be bothered by the other detectives passing in and out of Deborah's apartment.

"How tall again?" he asked a young policewoman who'd just seen her first dead body.

"Five-four," the youthful voice answered, with a touch of a break.

"Age?"

"Twenty-three, according to the driver's license."

"I'll want that checked," Karlov replied. "Remember, a license is the most easily obtainable document." Always the teacher, always the authority, he gently shook his pen at the policewoman. "Sex, F," he said out loud, filling in the appropriate blank. His voice had that doomsday quality that made even a letter of the alphabet sound like the end of the world. They said he sounded like Henry Kissinger, without the accent.

Now he glanced down at a transparent bag he had placed near his right shoe. It was tagged *Exhibit C.* He transferred that designation to a space at the bottom of his form. Inside the bag was a small papier-mâché gondola, like the ones in Venice. Unexceptional, except that it had been found resting at the head of Deborah Moore.

"I don't want this one leaked to the press either," Karlov ordered the policewoman. "I know what this is all about."

Everyone in the apartment knew what he meant. Another girl had been found murdered in her apartment the week before, also with a gondola at her head, but Karlov hadn't mentioned the gondola to the press. He'd guessed it was a sign, a code the killer might be using to taunt the police.

Now he knew he was right. He also suspected he had a serial murderer on his hands—someone who'd kill again and again, always leaving that little gondola, the symbol of his work, the signature of his art. And Karlov was frightened, more frightened than he'd ever been in his two decades with the department, for this murderer had a daring that Karlov had never seen in a serial killer before.

"Everything was mellow," Karlov said to the policewoman, thinking out loud.

She barely replied. She'd heard about Karlov's monologues, heard that he didn't expect an answer. It was his way of sorting out the facts.

"Both girls found in Manhattan apartments with puncture wounds in their chests," he continued, practically talking into space. "Yet, not one sign of anything out of place. These girls let their attacker in. They knew him. They probably *liked* him."

The slim blond policewoman raised her eyebrows, as if questioning what Karlov was saying.

"Look over there," Karlov said to her, a touch pendantically. He gestured toward a coffee table in the living room, clearly visible, although one of its legs was blocked by the victim's body. "Two glasses of Diet Coke on that table. Still fizzing. Fingerprints wiped from one. If you check the kitchen cabinets you'll see she used her best glasses. But she also had cheaper glasses and plastic cups. She liked this man."

Finally, the policewoman felt compelled to speak. She thought she had a logical point, something with which to impress Karlov, to get some credit. "If he knew both girls," she said with hesitation, "if you ask their friends—"

"We're bound to come up with the man's name," Karlov interrupted.

The policewoman nodded.

"It's the obvious solution," Karlov sighed, not meaning to put the young woman down, "but I have to assume he's smarter than that. He's careful. Meticulous. He vacuumed. He even washed the murder weapon."

"Washed the . . . ?"

Karlov smiled. He loved to give a virtuoso performance for a woman. He raised his hands, displaying his fingertips. "Sense of touch," he said. "One of the great weapons against crime." He gestured toward the dishwasher, clearly wanting the policewoman to touch it. She did. It was warm.

"It was probably turned on after the woman was killed," Karlov explained. "I think we'll find that one of the knives in there was the murder weapon. He washed it, along with all the victim's dishes. He'd make a wonderful husband.''

There was a sudden commotion at the front door as a squad of uniformed policemen burst in, escorting a doctor from the coroner's office. When he saw the field of blue, Karlov seemed to freeze. Then he took a step back, as a tension, a flash of fear, crossed his face. Curious, the policewoman thought. *Him* . . . scared of something? *Him* . . . the guy who's brought in the most beastly murderers in the city?

*   *   *

Leonard Anthony Karlov, born Leonid Antonin Karlovsky, who had gone from foot patrolman to high-ranking detective, had a deep, incurable fear of policemen.

Karlov was born in the United States, in Brooklyn in fact, but his parents had struggled out of Russia in the 1930s. They spoke no English when their only child was born, so they gave him a traditional Russian name. Later, they told him stories about Russia—first in Russian, then in the English they'd started to learn. Stories about men in greatcoats with badges and clubs, who came in the middle of the night and asked no questions before hauling their victims away. One of the victim's had been Karlov's father, a political prisoner long before the term became fashionable. Although Karlov had developed an interest in becoming a cop—it was a quick way out of his family's poverty—he still dragged the baggage of those childhood stories.

He was 42 now, single, convinced that marriage meant leaving a widow and kids when his number came up. He lived in a tiny rent-controlled apartment in the Riverdale section of the Bronx. His mother still lived in Brooklyn. His father had vanished without a trace in 1963. It was the

KGB, Karlov had told himself, although he couldn't figure out why.

He had a slim, almost Latin face—not at all Russian. A short nose. Deep brown eyes, long eyelashes and a warm smile.

The turmoil, the nightmares of his parents' background, the fear of authority—those he kept bottled inside, like a child's secrets.

* * *

He walked back into the living room, where the doctor from the coroner's office was completing his observations. Karlov knew Harold Kramer, MD, the smallish, pudgy forensic pathologist, known for his eagerness to get to any murder site. He liked him. Kramer was all cop inside. Sure, he'd pretend this was all for the advancement of science, but in truth the elfish physician relished the hunt, the logic of pursuit that was the stuff of any homicide case. Medicine was for plumbers.

"Find anything?" Karlov asked as Kramer made some notes.

Kramer looked up. "Oh, hello, Len. There's nothing here you don't know. Clean thrust to the heart, just like the last one. Not cuts on the fingers. You can read the thing the same way I can. She didn't defend herself. Didn't have time."

"Did she suffer?" Karlov asked. It was an odd question for a detective, but he was unusual—he felt for victims.

"No," Kramer replied. "It was almost instant." Then Kramer looked around, realized there were ears on the eight or nine cops in the room, and gestured for Karlov to walk to the bedroom. Karlov did, almost tripping over a speaker wire hooked to the hi-fi system. He and Kramer entered the bedroom, and Kramer closed the door.

"I heard about the little boat," Kramer said.

"The gondola?"

"Right. You have leads?"

"You kidding?" Karlov asked. "We just discovered the second gondola tonight. There'll be more, and it's complicated."

Kramer raised his eyebrows.

"They were both pointed in the same direction," Karlov said. "Almost due west."

"Coincidence?" Kramer asked.

"No. Both at the head, both west. I measured it on a compass. He's telling us something."

"Of course. You're saying it's a he. You sure?"

"Ninety-five percent," Karlov replied. "There were footprints in the carpeting. He couldn't hide them even with the vacuuming. He had to step out of the apartment. They're men's. Size nine-C. I can't guarantee they're his, but I'll go on that for now."

There was silence for some seconds, silence broken only by the muffled horns on the city streets outside, the buzzing of the policemen in the living room and the more distant murmuring of neighbors, who had congregated in the hall for the second murder in the building in four years.

Karlov looked at Kramer, contemplating the few facts known about the murders. He towered over him, the large, brooding Russian against the little doctor who only wished he wore Karlov's badge.

Kramer gestured to speak, but Karlov raised his hand. "I've already heard it," Karlov said. "He knew them both, so friends or relatives might know *him*."

"Yeah."

"It won't work out that way."

They walked back into the living room, the wooden floors creaking in the hallway, as they usually do in these pre-World War II West Side buildings. The living room, about twelve by eighteen, was decorated with modern but inexpensive furniture. Lots of black and white. The apartment was typical for a young woman in Manhattan.

Deborah Moore still lay there, covered by a sheet. Karlov bent down slowly, and gently lifted the sheet to take one last look at this second victim before Kramer had her carted away for the autopsy.

"I'll never foget their faces," Karlov said, to no one in particular. "They both looked so . . . surprised."

He covered her face again. "Next of kin?" he asked another detective.

"Notified," came the reply. "The mother."

Karlov turned away.

3

Although Karlov had his regular office at the main police headquarters in lower Manhattan, he set up temporary shop in the Twentieth Precinct on Manhattan's West Side, so he could be close to the scene of the murders. The Twentieth, like much of Manhattan, went from very rich to very poor, with a crime rate somewhat higher than one would expect in a region where two-bedroom apartments sold for $300,000. It was urban denseness, block after block of high rises, low rises and brownstones, interrupted by familiar neighborhood stores and a proliferation of boutiques, many of which wouldn't last.

All police precinct houses are old. They may be new, glass and brick, but they're still old. They *look* old, they *feel* old. They inevitably get worn and battered very quickly. There is something about the police presence, the atmosphere, that calls for oldness, for the conjuring of city streets with gaslight, for red-eyed Irish sergeants sitting at raised desks, their double chins quivering as they pronounce the law. And so the Twentieth Precinct headquarters looked old, although it had been built less than a decade before to be a "modern" precinct house for a modern department. Outside was the familiar parade of patrol cars that stand guard at any precinct house, waiting to be called.

Karlov's temporary office was on the second floor, a bare room with a gray service desk, metal visitors' chairs, and windows covered with a protective layer of grime. He had requested only one amenity—a blackboard, which he used to write down the pattern of his investigation to anyone who wanted to hear. And there was only one personal touch—small portraits of his mother and father, both taken soon after they arrived in America, which he kept on the desk. Not a day went by when Karlov didn't wonder what actually had happened to his father, but he had long ago given up calling Missing Persons or the FBI, neither of which had been much help.

The story of the second murder hit the newspapers. The *New York Post* screamed: SECOND GIRL KNIFED TO DEATH. To the left of the headline was a picture of Deborah Moore, and, underneath, a photo of Elizabeth Taylor with a new escort. It was a wonderful day for the *Post*.

The paper lay on Karlov's desk. But also before him was a roomful of people, divided neatly down the middle, all sitting on chairs commandeered from other offices. Next to Karlov, his legs spread slightly apart to accommodate his extra weight, was Dr. Harold Kramer. He'd asked to come to this meeting because, he'd told Karlov, something of medical importance might come up. Karlov knew it was a crock. It always was. Kramer was hooked on the case.

Most faces in the room were in their twenties, a few in their thirties. Glum. Tense. Expectant. People not used to the mustiness and spareness of a police precinct.

"I've asked you to come because you knew two people," Karlov began, looking around the room. "Those of you to my left knew Constance Rainey. You on the right knew Deborah Moore. What the papers say is true. They were both killed in the same way within days of each other. By having you all in the room we might be able to detect some common thread, maybe an activity they were doing together, something that ties it up. That okay with you all?"

There were the usual nods. Who would say no?

"Right here is Dr. Harold Kramer from the coroner's office. He did both autopsies. I'll tell you now that nothing unusual came up. Oh, by the way, the family wants you to know that Deborah Moore's funeral will be Thursday, here in New York. The sergeant at the desk has the details."

Karlov could sense the tension rising. Words like "autopsy" and "funeral" have an electric effect, which is precisely what he intended. He wanted these people to be serious, to bleed out information, not to think they could stay an hour, then jump to a downtown lunch.

"Now," Karlov went on, taking a set of three-by-five cards from his top metal drawer, "Sandra Shore."

"Yes?" a soft voice replied. It belonged to a young woman in the first row, a redhead wearing a blue business suit. She looked at Karlov apprehensively, as if she'd done something wrong.

"People say you were Constance Rainey's best friend," Karlov said.

The woman nodded.

"For how long?"

"Since high school. We came to New York together from Philadelphia."

"Stayed in very close touch?"

"Yes."

"How come you didn't live together?"

"We did, but I got married two years ago, then divorced. We just didn't get back together."

"Tell us about her."

Sandra Shore took a deep breath. Tears welled up in her eyes. She fought to keep control. Young, successful women are supposed to be cool, but the image of her best friend, whose body she'd identified at the morgue, froze in her mind. "She worked at a radio station in publicity," she said. "She was creative, always at museums, and she liked photography. She'd bought a Nikon camera recently."

"Boyfriends?"

"No one in particular."

"Popular?"

"Off and on. Connie wasn't that hot on getting married. She wanted some kind of career first. She worried about money."

"But she owned her own apartment."

"Her parents helped. She was actually thinking of selling it. It got very expensive. She talked about leaving New York. I just don't think she thought she'd make it here."

"She was unhappy?"

"No, just concerned about her future. There's so much pressure here."

"Attractive?"

"Yes. I'd say so. Warm. Connie was warm. You could talk to her."

* * *

Karlov went on, asking a number of routine questions, trying to get a portrait of the first girl who'd been murdered. But what emerged frustrated him, for Constance Rainey was like thousands of other young women in New York. There was not a single characteristic that stood out, that a detective could point to as a base from which to start an investigation.

He turned to Deborah Moore. He asked *her* best friend, Linda Dolen, a social worker, about her.

"She started out living in Queens," Dolen said, her voice shaking. "She moved to Manhattan recently and got the little co-op. I guess it was the same as the other girl. Her parents helped out. She worked on Wall Street and I think she told me her company gave her a loan to help, too. I can't believe she's gone. I was talking to her three days ago. I—"

"About what?" Karlov asked.

"About men. She wasn't thrilled with the guys she was meeting. The usual complaints."

"She go to singles bars?"

"Debbie? Never. It wasn't her style."

It hadn't been Constance Rainey's style either. In fact, both victims came off as a little old-fashioned and strait-laced.

As Karlov had predicted, no common names turned up at this session. Each person in the room was asked to draw up a list of the victims' friends, and no name appeared more than once. Of course, Karlov realized that someone in the room might be the murderer, but he seriously doubted it.

This killer was too smart to place himself in a vulnerable position. It was a gut hunch.

When the general discussion ended, Karlov tried something else. "I'm going to read you all a list of words," he announced. "If you think any of them is significant to your deceased friend, stop me."

He read from a three-by-five card. "Okay...naïve."

He looked around. No response.

"Religious."

Nothing again.

"Suspicious."

"Lonely."

"Scatterbrained."

The list went on. Sometimes some hands would go up when he mentioned words like "caring" or "affectionate," but he treated the responses skeptically. He knew that people always wanted to say something good about a murder victim.

Then he threw in one more.

"Italy."

It was for the gondolas.

There was no response.

"I want to thank you all for coming," he said, disappointed, abruptly ending the session. "You've been very helpful. I may call on you again."

"When do you expect to make an arrest?" asked a man toward the rear, in a tone that suggested Karlov and Kramer were his personal employees.

"After the next commercial," Karlov replied, sensing the man had been brought up on a mixture of "Kojak" and "Columbo."

But then he thought better. These people had known the victims. The answer had been out of line. "We're doing our best," he said, "but I won't make promises."

The room quickly emptied as everyone rushed to work. It had filled with cigarette smoke, which enveloped Karlov and Kramer in a haze, but they ignored it as a chronic hazard of police work.

* * *

"So?" Kramer asked.

"Zip," Karlov replied. "We're nowhere."

"We know that the girls knew the killer," Kramer countered.

"What else do we know? Just that in both cases he came in the front door of an apartment building and went upstairs," Karlov said. "We've checked all the residents. A few saw a man in Moore's building, but didn't know where he was going. We have the description, but it could've been anyone. No one saw anything with the first girl. As I said, zip."

"You think *anything* is important, aside from the gondolas?" Kramer asked.

"Wheel marks," Karlov replied cryptically.

"Come again."

"Vacuum cleaners leave wheel marks. In Deborah Moore's apartment there were more wheel marks near the TV than anywhere else in the room."

"So?"

"Maybe he had to clean up something near the TV," Karlov theorized.

"Something he spilled?"

"I don't know. But I'm interested in those wheel marks."

4

Third girl slain! Shouted the headline of the ever-restrained *New York Post*. The paper was on the street within ninety minutes after the body was discovered, just as Karlov was arriving on the scene.

Karlov felt ashamed. Helpless.

Humiliated.

Three murders, three innocent young women, obviously killed by the same man, a man who left a westward-pointed little gondola at the heads of his victims. Karlov hadn't gotten to square one. It was a pathetic, disgraceful situation. He'd been reduced to waiting around for others to die so that some new clue would come his way.

Marie Gould was her name.

In her twenties. Single. A one-bedroom apartment in a no-doorman building on the West Side. The usual pattern.

Again, Karlov examined the murder scene with his

usual thoroughness. Marie's face had that surprised look he'd noticed before. The girl hadn't been ready to die. She hadn't expected it. The killer *must* have been a friend who struck suddenly. It seemed the logical explanation for a series of murders with no logic and no apparent connection between the victims.

The dishwasher hadn't been turned on this time. Maybe the killer had taken the weapon with him.

Harold Kramer arrived, puffing heavily from carrying his weight around in the heat. He entered Marie Gould's living room, decorated with aging hand-me-downs from her family, examined the body and ordered it sent to the morgue. He discounted in advance the prospect that the autopsy would turn up anything.

The press waited outside the apartment. Both Karlov and Kramer feared there would be an inquisition in the press, an orgy of headlines and editorials that could shake public confidence in the police generally and in Leonard Karlov in particular.

"This will explode," Kramer told Karlov in Marie Gould's bedroom. "The mayor will open his very loud mouth. You've got terror in the city. Girls are afraid to open their doors."

Karlov didn't respond. He knew all that. He simply stood there in his dark brown suit—the uniform he wore all year round, even on the hottest days—and gazed around the bedroom. "Vacuumed," he said.

"So?" Kramer asked. "So was the last one."

"In the last one the living room was vacuumed. Here it's the bedroom." He continued to gaze around, noting a television set on its stand and some old oak furniture.

"Maybe it wasn't the killer who did the vacuuming," Kramer said. "Maybe she did. Maybe she was expecting some action in here and cleaned up.'' Kramer shrugged, his excess shoulders squeezing the flesh on his neck into ripples.

"He did the vacuuming," Karlov replied quietly.

"Come on," Kramer said.

Kramer remained expressionless. It was just one more clue, just one more revelation that did more to confuse than illuminate. "She was left-handed," he told Kramer. "It was on a medical form in her desk. But the cord was wrapped around the vacuum the way a right-handed person would wrap it."

"Maybe she had a housekeeper," Kramer shot back, trying to be useful, to prove that he too could detect.

"The housekeeper would have cleaned both rooms," Karlov said.

"Examine the contents of the vacuum bag," Kramer suggested.

"He took it with him, just like last time," Karlov answered matter-of-factly. "He even ran water through the tubes and cleaned the brushes."

"And he washed the knife the last time," Kramer recalled. "He's obsessed with neatness."

"Either that or he wanted to clean something for some specific reason. The wheel marks are heaviest near the TV set again, but that may just be coincidence. Or maybe they were sitting on the rug and watching TV, and they dropped crumbs or something. I'm guessing.

"He also has tremendous confidence," Karlov continued. "He's a thinker. Imagine, he killed these girls, then stayed long enough to do the rugs. I've never seen that. Usually they just run. This man is thoroughly convinced he can't be caught. He even leaves his calling card."

Kramer knew that Karlov was referring to the mysterious little gondolas.

"Hey, maybe he's a vacuum-cleaner salesman, the kind who put on demonstrations."

Karlov just stared at Kramer, with an icy put-down stare that told him this theory was too obvious. A smart killer doesn't advertise his profession.

"You think you'll get him?"

"I don't know. A lot of serial murderers never get caught."

"But it's the city," Kramer said. "This guy must've been *seen*."

"He probably was. But it *is* the city. People see. They look right through other people. Unless he was unusual, they don't notice. Or they don't come forward. All we have is a pattern. Three women in their twenties. All attractive. All single. All living alone. All in older buildings without doormen. All owned their apartments, even if it was a struggle. All let their attacker in. All apparently entertained him. All died with a single thrust to the chest. All were apparently surprised and couldn't put up a struggle. All were found with that little Venetian gondola at their heads, pointing in the same direction. All had that typical New York transient quality. You have the feeling they weren't going to stay long, or maybe that they just came. And yet there's no apparent motive."

"Maybe they're not the women we think they were," Kramer said.

"You might be right," Karlov conceded, wiping a bead of sweat from his receding brow. "My father told me about a circus clown in Moscow—a buffoon, a real fool who no one took seriously. It turned out he was a colonel in the KGB. Utterly ruthless. He sent thousands to their deaths. You just never know who someone really is. God knows who these women were. God knows if their friends or relatives really knew."

"Maybe it's international," Kramer said.

"Could be. Could be anything."

He and Kramer walked back to the living room. A police photographer with a Leica M-4P was just finishing his coverage of the crime scene. The flashes bothered Karlov. He'd always had sensitive eyes. He had to wear heavy sunglasses outside in bright weather.

Again he ordered his crew not to mention the gondola to the press. One reporter had found out but agreed to leave it out of his stories. Karlov noted the reporter's name. He'd have to return the favor. That's how the system worked.

He was about to leave when he stooped down to retrieve the gondola and place it in a plastic evidence bag. Then he noticed something.

Papier-mâché gondola.

Papier-mâché.

Paper.

Print.

5

For Laura Barnett, it was all too close.

She also lived in a West Side apartment. She also lived alone. She also was in her twenties. Every morning she fearfully turned first to the newspaper reports on the murder probe and read the latest news from the police—"investigation continuing," "tracking down leads," "fully expect success."

Success?

She'd heard the sirens when the last woman was murdered. She'd seen the flashing lights as patrol cars raced to the murder scene. She'd heard the first radio reports on WCBS that it had happened again. She'd picked up the chatter on the streets, from the guy at the newsstand, from a doorman down the block, from a delivery boy. Another killing. Another one close by. The guy knew the neighborhood. He had to. Why else would he concentrate his slaughters here? Maybe he worked in one of the stores where Laura Barnett shopped. Maybe she knew him. Maybe she talked to him.

What did they mean when they said "success"? How many more women had to die before they got the murderer? Laura was beginning to wonder about the police. What were they overlooking?

Laura was small, with short brown hair. She had a mellow, girlish face. Her blue eyes were roundish and oversized, her most prominent features, the kind of eyes that seemed to flash in each ray of light.

She'd always been careful. Now she was vigilant, determined not to open her door unless Glen was with her.

No, she told herself, she wasn't about to become some maniac's victim. Things were going too well. Glen was in her life now. She'd waited for him, dreamed of him even before she knew him. Nothing would interfere with this dizzying romance that had overwhelmed her—no disapproving relatives, no questioning friends, certainly not some serial murderer.

She felt she had everything to live for. For the first time in her life she felt totally optimistic. Love in a New York summer. No gloom. No depression. No self-pity. "I'm the luckiest person in the world," she had told Glen.

She glanced out the window of her eighth-floor, one-bedroom apartment. It was a balmy Saturday and the sidewalks were crammed with people strolling toward Central Park. She could see two break-dancing demonstrations, and two steel-drum bands. Business was good. The commerce of the street was booming. She could even smell the hot dogs, cooked by vendors, that sold for a dollar, including enough sauerkraut and mustard to guarantee a dry-cleaning bill. The people below seemed oblivious to the three murders, although Laura knew that many had to be talking about them, pointing out the buildings where they had happened.

* * *

The phone rang. A muted, electronic ring that came from the new phone Glen had given her. It must be him, she thought, her heart welcoming the ring. He'd be late. Law clients always thought of their legal problems on Saturday mornings.

Laura raced to the phone, mounted on her bright yellow kitchen wall, and picked up. "Glen?"

"Ms. Barnett?" came the unknown female voice at the other end. Not Glen.

"Uh . . . yes," Laura answered, a bit embarrassed.

"This is classified," the voice said. "I'm just checking the apartment ad you placed with us."

"Fine."

"Let me read you the copy, exactly as it will appear. Ready?"

"Yes."

"Under the headline 'Sunny Three . . .' "

Laura laughed. "Well, if you stand in the living room at the right angle . . ."

"It's okay," the woman said. "Everyone exaggerates. Now, after 'Sunny Three.' Quote, 'Bright one-bedroom on West Eighty-fourth Street. Entrance hall. Modern kitchen. Dishwasher. Elevator building. Block from park. 162-5282. Priced to sell.' Unquote."

"That's fine," Laura said.

"Now, Ms. Barnett, this will run next Friday, Saturday and Sunday for a package rate of sixty-two forty-five."

"Okay."

"Do you want to extend the run? We could give you—"

"On no, not now. Let's see what kind of reaction I . . ." Laura paused. A thought crossed her mind. It was inevitable in the circumstances.

"Ma'am," the voice asked, "anything wrong?"

"I was wondering," Laura replied, sitting down on one of the two barstools in her kitchen, playing with the bottle opener, "whether I can make a little change."

"Of course."

"Instead of just 'elevator building,' please say, 'safe elevator building.' "

"Yeah," the voice answered. "I can see why you'd want to say that . . . up there."

The comment was wounding. It was accurate, but still wounding. No one likes to be told that her neighborhood is a combat zone. "I would say it anyway," Laura countered. "I think it's important."

"The change is made," the voice answered. "Good luck in selling."

"Thank you." Laura hung up.

She gazed around her living room. All right, it wasn't elegance. It was a mix of family-contributed traditional and store-bought modern, the best she could afford as an assistant marketing manager for a small watch company.

But this apartment had seen so much, been so much a part of her life for six years. She remembered the day, only a week after graduating from NYU, when she went apartment hunting—scared, intimidated, always looking down at her hands, stained with the ink of crumpled real-estate ads. She remembered the rude agents who'd obviously thought she didn't have the rent money. She remembered finding the apartment, asking her parents to co-sign for the $745 rent, moving in with only a bed and night table.

She'd seen the building turn co-op, forcing out old people who'd been there a generation. She'd watched as they left, casualties of the real-estate machine that consumed Manhattan in the late seventies and early eighties. She'd managed a down payment only with family help and a backbreaking loan.

* * *

Her years in the apartment had been mixed. For before Glen entered her life there'd been Jason, and the only real terror Laura had ever known.

She remembered his voice. His angry face, so full of anguish.

She knew the words . . . by heart. She trembled as she heard them again.

"I'll kill myself," he'd cried. "You're a witch."

She'd known he'd take it hard when she said good-bye, but she hadn't been ready for just *how* hard.

She remembered his grabbing her arm and shaking her. *"Not good enough for you?"*

Those eyes burned. He was a cultured, educated man, an assistant professor of art at Columbia, but there was this other side, this unstable side.

"You're going for the money, aren't you? You want cash on the line. No schoolteachers for you. Right? *Right?*"

Neighbors had heard the shouting. Afraid he was hurting her, one even called the police.

She'd tried to be gentle, but it simply had to end.

But even after it did, he'd kept calling.

"I tried to slash my wrists today," he once told her. She'd known it wasn't true. Jason had always been a romantic, full of hyperbole. "I've got a gun," he told her. "One shot, and my agony is over." She knew he was making it up, trying to play on her sympathies.

One time he'd showed up at her building and she made the mistake of letting him in. She'd reasoned that she could talk to him, make him understand that there was life after Laura Barnett. He couldn't be convinced, but finally he just cursed at her and left. She never saw him again, though she knew he still taught at Columbia. He did send her a Christmas card, coldly signed ''the only artist you'll ever know.''

She kept the card although she couldn't understand why. Maybe it was a reminder of how bad things had been with Jason, of the contrast between Jason and Glen. Maybe it *would* be good to get out of this apartment, away from the memories of the twisted man who couldn't accept defeat.

She went to the window again, as if looking for Glen would make him arrive sooner. As she looked down she noticed a red Ford weaving its way through the dense traffic, its driver gazing out as if searching for an address. She quickly turned her attention back to the crowds.

Laura walked back from the window and brushed her hair. She shivered without knowing why.

6

The air conditioning was working at the twentieth precinct, but Karlov knew it only by the rattling of the air vents and the dust shooting out of them. It hadn't been serviced in two years, and he felt the sweat coating his neck as he stood over a bathroom sink.

He'd filled a small Fantus clothes steamer, the kind people take on trips to get wrinkles out of clothes, and was letting it heat. In the sink was the small gondola he'd found near the first murder victim—Constance Rainey. The bathroom door was open, but lack of space forced Harold Kramer, MD, to wait outside, going through a police report on Marie Gould.

The steamer was supposed to take only a few minutes to steam, but to Karlov it seemed hours. He sensed he was on to something. He'd sensed it when he saw the little flap of paper sticking up from the gondola near Marie Gould's body, a flap that had come unstuck from the side of the little boat.

"Here's something," Kramer blurted out, jutting his finger into page six of the police report.

"What's that?" Karlov asked, more interested in watching for the first burst of steam from the steamer.

"This Gould woman, she was active in politics."

"So?"

"Says here she had meetings in her apartment."

"I read that," Karlov responded, his voice echoing off the bathroom walls, his breath causing a slight fogging of the mirror.

"A lot of people must've come," Kramer said, sitting down in a metal chair to study the report further. "Maybe one of them—"

"We've checked the list of all her political friends against lists from the other two murders," Karlov answered. "Nothing matches. I'm not saying you're wrong. It could be someone from a political group. It could also be Western Union."

"Come again?"

"Western Union, or someone you'd open the door for."

"They have ID," Kramer countered.

"Anyone can get ID." Karlov recalled an FBI agent's theory that his father had been spirited away by someone with false ID. He'd always been amazed how people believe any card with a picture on it. "There was a case in Jersey a couple of years ago. Kids were being snatched outside school by some guy in a car. Turned out he was using a badge and telling them he was a cop. He said their mothers were hurt and he was there to get them. The badge came from a toy store."

"This wasn't a kid," Kramer said. "This Marie Gould."

"We're all kids sometimes," Karlov answered. "Hal,

people are gullible. You're a doctor. You like details and facts and proofs, like in geometry. Most people believe anything."

"Even in New York?"

"Especially in New York. Anything can be believed here."

Kramer continued reading the report. He rarely argued a point with Karlov. He respected Karlov's experience, his European intellect, his love of logic. Harold Kramer was vastly better educated than Karlov—a BA from Tufts, an MD from Michigan—but he detected in Karlov that deeper intelligence, that brooding intellect that comes more from the burning experiences of life than from books. Karlov had gone to City University for two years, then dropped out, tried a few courses at John Jay College of Criminal Justice, but just hadn't had the patience for the classroom. The lack of a degree had held him back—one efficiency report commented on his minimal schooling—but his success rate countered the impact. He never resented those more educated than he was, never felt he was competing with them. His parents had wanted him to be a lawyer, but their reverence for formal training never really rubbed off.

If he hadn't been a policeman, he probably would've been an inventor. A gadget could occupy him for an entire afternoon, even if he had no real idea how it worked, or why.

"Steam," Karlov said. He looked down at the head of the electric steamer, which looked like the floor-cleaning attachment of a vacuum cleaner, with little vents where the steam flowed out.

Now Kramer put the report down and walked to the entrance of the bathroom. The paint was chipping off the walls, and one of the bulbs was out, but Kramer hardly noticed, entranced as he was by Karlov's experiment.

Slowly, Karlov picked up the small gondola in his left hand. He moved the steamer toward it and stroked the boat up and down.

"Nothing's happening," Kramer said.

"Do you do an autopsy in ten seconds?" Karlov replied.

Kramer didn't answer. He didn't quite see this performance as an autopsy.

Then, slowly, a piece of paper started melting away from the gondola. As it did, a bit of the inside showed. Plain newspaper. Karlov had assumed it. When he was young his father had built a model racing-car track, and used papier-mâché for hills and platforms.

Kramer inched closer, his heavy breathing contributing to Karlov's discomfort. They were like two photographers watching an image come up in a darkroom, an image that might reveal some lost secret, some elusive fact that would open up the case of the three murdered women.

Karlov continued applying steam to the gondola, his left hand feeling the heat and turning partly red, the glue from the small boat dripping into the sink and staining the porcelain. Suddenly, a full strip of paper melted off. Karlov put down both gondola and steamer, and picked up the strip. It was an ad for a Chevrolet. Three thousand dollars. "An oldie," Karlov said, and started steaming again.

One by one, other strips melted away, revealing the wire mesh frame of the little Venetian model. One strip fell flatly into the sink. Karlov and Kramer stared at it, and instantly realized they'd hit something.

What they saw were the words *Chicago Daily News*. Under it was the date. The precise date was missing—there was a hole in the paper—but the month was clearly June. And the year was 1964.

"Chicago," Karlov muttered. "He could've been there, or lived there."

"You think the gondola is from 1964?" Kramer asked.

"Maybe. Or, it could be from a few weeks ago. There are people who store old papers." But then he carefully examined the strip of newsprint, which had been coated with glue. "This paper wasn't lying around," Karlov said. "It's still white, protected from the air. I'll make an educated guess. The gondola was made in 1964."

"In Chicago," Kramer said.

"That I don't know. What if he was in, say, Los Angeles, and had Chicago papers sent to him. Maybe he'd been *from* Chicago."

"Fingerprints?"

"I doubt it. The glue probably soaked them out." But he placed every remnant from the gondola in a plastic bag, wondering if some piece of thread, something, might be found that would help him. "Look at this," he said, pointing at a second strip of paper. "Story on Barry Goldwater, almost sure to be the Republican nominee. Why would anyone carry these things around for twenty years? They're amateur models, not the store-bought kind. The type of stuff kids make. This guy's had at least three . . . for twenty years."

"Maybe he made them, had them in the attic," Kramer suggested.

"Yeah. But why leave them at murder sites?"

Kramer just shrugged.

"How many does he have?" Karlov asked. "As many as he needs for every murder he plans?"

"Maybe he'll start leaving something else," Kramer suggested.

Both men knew they were blowing smoke. Everything was theory. Added to what they knew about the murders—which wasn't much—was the fact that one gondola was fabricated more than two decades before, of newspapers from Chicago. The information, Karlov knew, could be of profound importance, or not important at all. He had to go further. He had the other two gondolas, and, although the DA's office was uneasy about dismantling evidence, Karlov had convinced them that it was absolutely essential.

* * *

And so the ritual was carried out once more. Karlov steamed the second gondola apart. And once more Harold Kramer was with him, observing, concerned that Karlov would burn his left hand with the steamer, intrigued by the bits of ancient history that floated into the police sink.

The second gondola revealed a second Chicago newspaper—June 4, 1964. There was a picture of Senator Hubert Humphrey of Minnesota, part of an article speculating on whether Lyndon Johnson would choose him as his vice presidential nominee at the upcoming Democratic convention. But, aside from the different news stories, nothing was revealed that hadn't been revealed in taking apart the first gondola.

The third gondola was the same.

Another part of the *Chicago Daily News*.

Same day.

Intrigued by the age of the newspapers, Karlov walked back to his office, carrying plastic bags filled with the dismantled evidence. When he arrived he found a copy of the *New York Post* on his desk, with the headline, LOCK YOUR DOORS! The Post was having a field day with the murders of the three girls, and was following the hallowed tradition of summer journalism: when news gets slow, announce a crime wave. And yet, Karlov grudgingly admitted the headline was good advice. Three women had opened their doors to the wrong man. If the wild headline would alert other women to the danger, maybe a murder could be averted. Or two. Or three.

Like most senior detectives, Karlov knew key men in other departments, including Chicago's. He grabbed his personal address book, flipped to a page, then reached for his phone.

7

The repairman got out of the red Ford and checked the signs to be sure he was legally parked. Do nothing, he told himself, that would link the car to the neighborhood. He even walked back to be sure the Ford was close enough to the curb and more than twenty feet from the fire hydrant in front of it. Precision, neatness, were his trademarks.

He rubbed his right ear, while feeling the sudden temptation to walk past the buildings where he'd murdered the last three. He started toward one, on West Seventy-eighth. He stopped. No, don't do it. Every detective knows the old saw that the criminal always returns to the scene of the crime. The police probably had plainclothesmen posted near those buildings, watching, waiting, looking into the eyes of those who passed. So the repairman started toward *her* building, melting in among the strollers, donning his sunglasses, not to keep out the glare, but to hide his face.

He walked slowly down her block, almost hit by a kid

who insisted on riding his two-wheeler on the sidewalk. Funny, the repairman thought—after all the plans, all the shrewdness, all the details, it would be funny if he got killed right here. But he kept walking, observing everything, making mental notes of the little things he had to know: No doorman at the front entrance to her building. Small lobby. Two elevators off to the side, both apparently working. Staircase to the right, leading to a doctor's office. No streetlight in front of the entrance. Most important, no signs saying the block is patrolled. Those signs were posted when there were private security guards.

He saw no obvious problems. Everything was in order.

There was a heavy-set man sitting on the steps of a brownstone across the street slurping an ice-cream cone, a Coke beside him. The repairman crossed the street and stood beside the man for a few moments, as if surveying the territory. Then he turned to him. "Lots of traffic around here at night?" he asked.

The man looked up at him, a little curious. New Yorkers are surprised to be approached by strangers, sometimes even by friends. "Nope," he replied. "Quiet at night. Too quiet if y'ask me. We had some action a year ago when they were fixin' the next street. We caught the extra traffic. Y'know?"

"Sure."

"You thinkin' of movin' here?"

"Yeah."

"Prices are ridiculous. You shoulda come five years ago."

"Yeah. It's a safe neighborhood, though," the repairman said.

"Oh yeah? For the muggers maybe. Our ethnic friends, y'know what I mean?"

"I know."

"Not good at night. No one goes out. Y'could look up and down this block, maybe see ten people an hour. It's the truth."

"That's too bad," the repairman replied. "Maybe it's not for me."

"Wait for the depression."

The repairman laughed. "Well, thanks," he said, and started walking. All the signs continued positive. There was nothing about this block to deter him.

The repairman carried a blue L. L. Bean shoulder pouch, the kind hunters use. He unzipped its large compartment and fingered a gift-wrapped box inside.

8

Glen *was* a little late now, and it was natural for Laura to worry. Images flashed through her mind of rich, overbearing clients harassing him, boring him with their little problems, their obsessions, their fantasies and paranoia. Glen's ambivalence toward law stemmed from having to represent so many people he couldn't stand. He often joked about charging not by the hour, but by the cubic feet of cigar smoke blown in his face.

Laura called Glen's number. No answer. Good. He was on the way.

They met at a business seminar. Laura had hoped to make some contacts that would lead to new sales, Glen had come to escape his loneliness. Comfortable with the certainty of numbers and statistics, Laura had been skeptical of lawyers, with their flair for orchestrating confusion. But Glen turned out to be a straight shooter, and seemed calm, unlike Jason. It worked from the first night.

The buzzer in Laura's kitchen rang. It had to be Glen, at the building's front door, waiting to be let in. She felt a spark of excitement as she rushed to the intercom and threw the "Talk" switch.

"Yes?"

"Package for Laura Barnett," the voice said, faint and almost mumbling.

Disappointment. It wasn't Glen. "Can you deliver it?" she asked.

"No way. Gotta leave it by the door, ma'am."

"But—"

Click.

Typical. Delivery men hated to come upstairs. Lost time. Extra work. And some people never bothered to tip. So, Laura left the apartment and rode down in the elevator, wondering who'd left the package. She'd been expecting a suit from Bloomingdale's. That had to be it.

But when she got downstairs she discovered a little gift-wrapped box, too small for a suit. It was lying in the vestibule between the door to the hallway and the door to the street. Rude, Laura thought. Anyone could take it. She wondered how many packages she'd never received because they simply disappeared from the vestibule. She picked it up.

*　　*　　*

He noticed *her.*

After all, that had been his objective, to stare at her, study her, assess her, evaluate her. It was the first time he'd ever done things quite this way—a change in his method of operation, an extra step to avoid wasting time on losers.

Yes, this was a good one.

Yes, the face matched that soft, mellow voice. And he loved those bright eyes.

Yes, she would join the list, even have priority over some of the others. This was good stuff, not to be missed or put off too long.

The repairman turned away as Laura started to return to the elevator. He walked down her block, feeling he had accomplished something, then stopped, bought a hot dog and Diet Coke, and watched a small steel band that had taken over a corner. He even tossed a buck into the hat that the band had placed out front, earning a thank-you nod from one of the players. Why not be generous? It had been a very good day. He walked to the red Ford, whose left front fender was now occupied by a neighborhood resident with a large radio, and courteously told the music lover that he was the owner of the vehicle and was about to depart. The teenager jumped off the fender, and the repairman drove off.

*   *   *

Laura returned to her apartment and opened the small box, from which all fingerprints had been wiped, and whose inside had been vacuumed to eliminate incriminating fibers. The gift was a pound of candy with a card saying, *An admirer.*

She loved it. Glen always pulled these little jokes.

Glen arrived about ten minutes later. Laura buzzed him through the front door and waited as he came up by elevator.

She was at the door.

It was the longest kiss she could remember.

"Business?" she asked, as they separated to a total distance of six inches."

"Business."

"Tell me."

"Some client got a very nasty letter from the IRS. He wants me to bail him out of trouble. He thinks I'm a miracle worker."

"Can you bail him out?"

"No. He won't understand that he's committed fraud, that there's no way to hide it, that the best I can do is plead mitigating circumstances. He wants someone who'll get him the Congressional Medal of Honor."

Glen collapsed into an easy chair, worn down by his encounter with fiscal criminality. He'd begun his legal career as an assistant U.S. attorney, making little money but at least doing some good. He left for the same reason most left—to seek some financial security. Now he had it. He also had the feeling he was wasting time, pushing paper for clients who contributed nothing to society but the use of their credit cards.

But now he smiled over at Laura, that reassuring smile that told her no client, business, deal or cash could come between them. Glen had a quiet handsomeness—more scholar than tough guy, more persuader than fighter. He was medium height, beginning to loosen a bit about the middle, with a few strands of premature gray in his dark brown curly hair. He was thirty-one, but admitted to looking older. It helped in court. It hurt for life insurance.

He was wearing khakis, a solid blue sport shirt and Nike sneakers—standard combat dress for the West Side.

"Still want to go to the park?" he asked, stretching out his legs and leaning his head back.

"Sure. Don't you?"

"Yeah, but I was thinking—you want to rent some bikes?"

Pure romance, Laura thought. But then, just hearing a calm male voice was romantic enough after Jason. "Why not? But . . . look, I haven't ridden a two-wheeler since the fourth grade.''

"Oh."

"Guess I ruined it for you."

"Well, if you fall I can sue the city. We'll win, retire to the country, repair your broken leg . . ."

"Oh, hey, thanks. Yeah, thanks a lot."

"So you don't want to?"

"Can we go slow?"

"Sure," Glen answered. "And we'll go where there aren't too many riders. I'll get you back to it. Trust me."

"Sold."

Laura walked to a closet to get a light jacket. "Oh, by the way, thanks."

"Thanks?"

"Come on."

"No," Glen said. "Thanks for what?"

"For being . . . an admirer." She took the box of candy from a table. "Have some of your calories. They're good."

Glen sat up, baffled. "Laura, what the hell are you talking about?"

Laura knew there was something behind this. Glen was a great practical joker. "I'm talking about the candy," she replied. "It was downstairs, next to the mailbox . . ."

"So what? *I* didn't send it."

He meant it, Laura suddenly realized. She knew when he was serious, and now he was serious. It threw her. She wasn't expecting this. "You didn't—?"

"No."

Laura quickly put the candy back on the table, as if it were suddenly contaminated. "Glen, it arrived gift-wrapped, with this little card."

Glen studied the card. "Looks like I've got competition."

"Never."

"Never say never."

"But who? Everyone knows about us. Look, maybe it's a joke. One of our friends."

"Could be," Glen said. "Don't sweat it."

All right, Laura realized, it wasn't from Glen. And maybe it *was* a joke. But he was right. Why sweat it?

Then an awful thought crossed her mind. Jason playing a joke. She held it in. Why upset Glen? He'd had such a rotten morning. Let him enjoy the day.

He quickly leafed through a phone book and then dialed a number. "Hello, Alpha Cycles? I'd like to rent two bikes, one men's, one ladies'. Anything available?"

He nodded the okay to Laura as the salesman read off a list of available bikes and prices. Glen made the reservation.

They were soon ready to leave. Laura set her answering machine and turned out the lights. But Glen watched her, studied her, realized something was wrong. There was strain in her face, a tightness in her lips. "Something eating you?" he asked.

She didn't answer at first, lowering the blind in the living room. He kept watching her as she returned to him. She took a deep breath and glanced down at the innocent-looking box of candy. "Jason," she whispered.

"No," Glen said. "I can't believe—"

"You don't know him."

"Don't worry," Glen said, placing his arm around her. "If it is, I'll take care of him."

Suddenly, they both stared at the candy.

9

James Hurley was a Deputy Inspector in the Chicago
Police Department, retired. The "retired" was premature,
awkward and not something he particularly liked to discuss.
A consummate expert in murder, Hurley had also been an
expert in some of the lesser activities of Chicago police
officers, such as accepting gratuities from certain business
establishments. His retirement in 1981 had been sudden,
suggested by the district attorney, and discreet.

But as a detective he had been the best, and Karlov
often consulted him on tough cases or questions of police
precedure. Now, at fifty-six, he sat at home each day, almost
fearful of going out because of the stares of neighbors,
wondering how he could rebuild his shattered life, his
disgraced career. His tall figure was stooped, his abnormally
long neck beginning to curve, his white hair mussed. His
wife and grown sons had stood by him, but Hurley felt
embarrassed at family dinners. He was the man who had

tarnished the name, who had left a legacy that could only be discussed in whispers, who could not look his parish priest in the eye.

He lived in one of the dreary row houses near the old Chicago stockyards. The houses were impeccably neat, the pride of lower-middle-class homeowners who still scrubbed the stoops, swept the paths and kept their neighborhoods white. This had been the domain of Richard Daley.

Hurley was sitting in his worn living room reading the *Chicago Sun-Times* when the phone rang. A tiny, pained smile came to his face when he heard the voice at the other end. He hadn't spoken with Leonard Karlov in more than two years.

Karlov knew the story, knew of Hurley's disgrace, but felt the man still had value, still could perform some service, and should be treated with some respect.

"Len," Hurley said with the slight touch of Irish accent that remained, "nice to hear from you, Len. So nice. How's your mom?"

"She's fine, Jim," Karlov answered. Kramer was listening in as he spoke. Karlov, incredibly, took on some of the gestures and accents of an Irish cop. He'd become part Irish by osmosis, rather easy in a big-city department. Suddenly Karlov became animated, his eyes opening wide, his free hand swinging in broad gestures, his warm smile even more expanisve than it normally was. Kramer couldn't decide whether it was automatic or a put-on. Whatever, it was magnificently effective, making Karlov instantly acceptable to the leading police in-group. "And how is Florence?" he asked Hurley.

There was a pause. "Oh, she's . . . okay, Len," Hurley answered, the gloom choking his vocal cords.

"What do I hear?" Karlov asked.

Hurley sighed. "You know how it is, Len. Ever

since . . . the trouble, well, it's sad for her. She would've been better off with some other Joe.''

"Baloney," Karlov responded. He'd have liked to use stronger language, but knew that Hurley, despite his other corruptions, had never cursed. "She's married to a fine man and a fine cop. You can't harp on your little mistake forever, Jim. Y'really can't.''

"Sure, Len," Hurley answered, not really hearing, not really wanting to hear. "Sure, I understand."

"Now, Jim," Karlov went on, "I want you to listen to me carefully. I've got some important questions."

"Personal?"

"No, Jim, police. Homicide."

A slight tingle of electricity shot through the half-broken man. He was being asked. He was being consulted. He wasn't the untouchable. He sat up a bit in his chair. "You're havin' a problem," he said to Karlov.

"That's the understatement. Look, Len. I want you to think back to about 1964.''

"Sure."

"Does the word *gondola* mean anything to you?"

"*Gondola?*" Hurley asked. "Len, my head isn't sendin' me the right signal."

" A gondola, Jim. You know those little boats that go around Venice, in Italy?"

"Oh yeah. I saw snapshots of those things. We got a neighbor. He went there. Yeah, they row people around."

"That's right. Now Jim, little models of those boats are being left at homicides here. All young women. The boats are made of Chicago newspapers from 1964."

"Dear Mary."

"That's why I asked. Maybe there was something then."

"Lemme think," Hurley said. There was a long pause

while he tried to orient his mind to 1964. "No," he finally said, "I don't make a connection, Len. Now, I could forget. But somethin' like that—if some sucker'd put boats near homicides, I'd remember."

"Do you remember *anything* about gondolas from that period, Jim? Did some suspect make them as a hobby? Was there some homicide that was linked to Venice? Or Italy? Please think, Jim."

"Negative," Hurley replied. "But it's I-talian. There's lots of I-talian here. Maybe that was the connection."

"Maybe," Karlov said. "Jim, I'll check records on this, but you can give me a quicker answer. Do you remember any murders from the sixty-four period where girls let their attacker in, even entertained him? I'm talking about an intelligent murderer who left no tracks."

Hurley thought about it. "Well, I *do* remember a case," he said. "It may not be of any help."

"Describe it," Karlov requested.

"She was a girl in her twenties. About 1966. She let a guy in and she entertained him."

Karlov whipped out a pencil. Key words were flowing.

"She let him in and served him a soda," Hurley continued. "I'm sure I recall. Maybe it was 1966."

"Maybe 1964?" Karlov asked.

"May-be," Hurley answered. "It's *why* she let him in that got us for a while. He killed her. I think he used a cord. The neck, y'know."

"Why *did* she let him in?" Karlov asked excitedly.

"It was Halloween."

"Halloween?"

"He said his kid brother was sick, so he was out trick or treatin' for him. He tried that a couple of times. That's how we got him. Finally, some girl opened the door. I guess they got talkin'. God knows why he killed her. He didn't even know her.''

''Where is he now?'' Karlov asked.

''Where you think, cop?''

''Jesus. He's not . . . ?''

''Pulled an insanity plea. Six years in some shrink palace, then back on the streets. God knows what he's doin'.''

Karlov carefully wrote down everything Hurley said. It *was* possible that this man, who'd been in Chicago when the gondolas were made, was on the prowl again. It happened all the time that a criminal would show up years later using the same techniques.

''Jim,'' Karlov asked, ''did you actually *know* this man?''

''I met him,'' Hurley replied. ''I was brought into the third degree.''

''Was he neat?''

''Neat?''

''You know, clean. Careful about things.''

Hurley shrugged. ''Well, he did wipe all his fingerprints, if that's what you mean.''

''Did he clean up the homicide site?''

''Don't remember.''

''Do you remember his name?''

''I remember every killer's name. It was Everett Morton Howe. Fancy name. Came from a good home, like Leopold and Loeb. They were from Chicago, y'know.''

''I remember.''

''It was 1965,'' Hurley suddenly blurted.

''What?''

''That was the year he did it, Len. It was 1965. I remember because it happened the same night you had that big blackout in New York.''

"Not 1966?"

"Sixty-five."

"Jim, think back. This man, Everett Milton Howe . . ."

"Morton."

Karlov grinned, then winked at Kramer. He'd been testing Hurley's attention to detail. Hurley's mind was still there, still fulfilling the detective's creed that nothing be overlooked.

"Okay, Everett Morton Howe," Karlov continued, "was he ever involved in anything else?"

"No, he had no record," Hurley said. "But remember, Len m'boy, that means nothing, absolutely *nothing*."

Karlov knew what Hurley meant. No record meant no *known* record. Serial killers often went undetected. People would disappear, or be found dead, and their cases would never be solved. Victims of the same killer would never be linked.

"He used a cord to kill her," Karlov continued. "Was he packin' anything else?"

"Not that I recall," Hurley replied. "Think we're on to something, Len?"

"Maybe," Karlov answered. "If we are, it's your doing, Jim. If this is the man, and I get the collar, you'll be there. I mean that."

"Good God," Hurley whispered. There was a touch of hope in what Leonard Karlov was saying.

* * *

Their conversation ended. Karlov leaned back in his desk chair, which grunted under the strain. "Incredible how a hunch can pay off," he told Kramer. "The best computer is still the human mind." He gestured toward the bathroom, where the surgery on the gondolas had been performed. "It's amazing that a guy this careful never realized those gondolas could be taken apart. It nailed down the city . . . at least I think so. The fact that Hurley remembered a guy . . . from Chicago . . . about the time these little boats were made . . . conned a woman into letting him in . . . she entertained him . . .''

But Kramer shrugged. He couldn't see what all the excitement was about. ''Could be coincidence.''

Karlov froze, then slowly leaned forward. ''Don't you think I know that?'' he asked. ''It could be nothing. It could be that Jim Hurley didn't remember it right. It could be a lot of things. And it *could* be our man.''

''Yeah . . .'' Kramer answered, still hardly overwhelmed. He was tied to the logic of medicine, the idea that solutions are reached through precise formulas.

''The one thing I'm gonna teach you, Hal,'' Karlov went on, ''is never to turn your nose up at a lead. *Any* lead. And this is a damn sight hell of a lot better lead than ninety percent of 'em. I hope it works out. Not just to catch the guy—that's the most important thing—but maybe I can do something for Jim Hurley out there. I'd like that. I really would.''

*   *   *

Karlov and Kramer rushed downstairs to Karlov's own car, a green 1982 Chevrolet with its hubcaps removed. Karlov had police insignia above the license plate, and knew the life expectancy of hubcaps on a cop's car in New York City. The car also bore some gratuitous art work, generously donated by neighborhood kids and covered, more or less, by a body shop that did the work for Karlov at a civil-service discount.

The detective and forensic doctor raced downtown, dodging the taxis, trucks, catcalls and horns, and turned into the garage under One Police Plaza, a modern brick office building, main headquarters of the NYPD. Then they raced upstairs to a data processing room, where computer terminals were installed, linked to a nationwide crime information network. Karlov was well known in the room, which was the size of a small gymnasium. He used the information network often. It gave a modern look to the department, although he knew that relatively few cases were solved, or even advanced here.

Policewoman Emily Arthur, taller than either man, slim as a toothpick and wearing horn-rimmed glasses that made her look more like a psychiatrist than a cop, was assigned to help Karlov. Arthur was remarkably efficient, Karlov knew, but spoke in tones just above a whisper, almost blending in with the humming of the equipment. Karlov had to strain to hear her, but trusted her knowledge of the equipment and the information network to which it was attached. Besides, Arthur had a bit of special status. She was a descendant of President Chester Arthur, who'd been a minor New York politician before going on to what Karlov called "less exciting things."

"What can I do for you gentlemen?" Arthur asked, with only a touch of a smile. Karlov could see the computers reflected in her glasses.

"Emily, could you punch up Everett Morton Howe?" Karlov asked. "Please do it by name, also by homicide, also by criminal insanity."

Arthur just nodded, then sat down at a Hewlett-Packard keyboard with a small green screen just above it. "I'm sure you'll want a printout," she said, flipping a switch.

"Definitely," Karlov said.

The whole computer process was still a mystery to Karlov, though it was old stuff to Kramer. Karlov had mixed feelings about anything that compromised the romance of detection, yet he did not resist the new devices. He always insisted they would simply *supplement,* not supplant.

Emily Arthur, her long legs stretched out under the console, started punching in the information network. Everything she punched appeared on the screen, beginning with HOWE, EVERETT MORTON. After she was finished, they all waited, silently, mesmerized by the screen, as if it were some wise man about to deliver the answer to a deep, troubling question.

Finally, words started appearing.

HOWE, EVERETT MORTON, ARRESTED CHICAGO, ILL, 11/14/ 1965, MURDER 1 . . . TRIED, CHICAGO, ILL, NOT GUILTY, INSANITY . . . COMMITTED ILLINOIS STATE MENTAL FACILITY, CHICAGO, ILL, 3/3/1966 . . . RELEASED 6/16/1972.

The machine stopped. "I need more," Karlov said.
"More coming," Arthur assured him.
And the words started flowing again.

ARRESTED 3/31/1974, LOS ANGELES, CALIF, ATTEMPTED AGGRAVATED RAPE . . . TRIED LOS ANGELES, CALIF, NOT GUILTY, INSANITY . . . COMMITTED LOS ANGELES MENTAL HOSPITAL, LOS ANGELES, CALIF, 12/8/1974 . . . ESCAPED 8/14/1977 . . . SEVERAL SIGHTINGS ON EAST COAST . . . NO ARREST.

Again, the machine stopped. But, within a few seconds, it cut in again.

ADDENDA HOWE, EVERETT MORTON, APPREHENDED . . .

It stopped. Karlov and Kramer tensed, stared at it. Karlov feared that Howe had been apprehended and was no longer in circulation, canceling the lead, hurling the case back to zero.

But the machine continued . . .

APPREHENDED 11/14/1984, YONKERS, NEW YORK . . . RELEASED IN POLICE ID ERROR . . . END OF REPORT.

They'd had him.

They'd had him in Yonkers, but released him because of a police error. Common, Karlov knew. It happened all the time. But Everett Morton Howe was still loose, and the blunder had occurred just a few miles north of New York City.

It was a lead. It was something. Maybe he was the man. It was worth the shot.

Find him.

10

"**D**on't shake so much, friend," Karlov told the young patrolman, who sat rigidly on a steel chair in his office like some pupil who'd been caught skipping school. "It was an honest error. We're not here to hang you for it. I just want information."

"I'll try to help, sir," the patrolman said, his brow breaking out in heavy sweat. Patrolman Sean Finney was all of twenty-two, sandy-haired, with a tiny turned-up nose, like that of a kid in a cereal ad. He'd been with the Yonkers force less than two years. Good record. A few arrests. A full quota of parking tickets. But it was Finney who'd released Everett Morton Howe after stopping him for crossing a double white line on Warburton Avenue, near the Hudson River. All Karlov wanted was a detailed account of the incident, something that might give him some microscopic piece of information that would lead him to Howe, the escaped mental patient who'd killed a girl in Chicago in 1965.

"All right, he was proceeding north at thirty miles per hour," Karlov said. "You were two cars behind him and saw him cross the line. How many times?"

"Twice, sir."

"You don't have to call me sir."

"Twice. I thought he might be DWI—we're gettin' tough on drunks, sir. So I pulled around and stopped him."

"You make him exit the vehicle?"

"Yes, sir. But he didn't appear DWI. He looked familiar, though."

"How so?"

"I'd seen the face."

"Well, maybe he was living in Yonkers. You'd see his face."

"New Jersey plates, sir."

"Okay, you knew the face."

"I thought maybe it was from a 'wanted' bulletin. But so many faces look alike. Y'know, you don't want false arrest . . ."

"Sure."

"I quizzed him. He had all the right ID. I remember the name was Fred Slocum, Fair Lawn, N.J. But he seemed all right. Passed the mobile drunk test, and apologized for crossing the line. He said somethin' about a car tryin' to squeeze him on his right. Okay, man, it happens. There were pictures of some little kids in his wallet—y'know, I checked his license . . ."

"Yeah."

"So, I figured, what the hell. I coulda seen that face in a million places."

"You let him go."

Finney lowered his head, then shrugged. "Yeah. Sorry."

"It's okay. But later you realized he was hot property."

"Yeah. I saw his face on one of those circulars. I reported what happened. Y'gotta give me credit for that."

"I do," Karlov said, feeling for the young man. He'd once made a mistake like that when he was a young patrolman.

"I mean, I didn't try to cover up."

"I understand. I'm a cop, too. But when you checked the Slocum name, you found out there was no one by that name in Fair Lawn."

"Right, and the license didn't check out either. All phoney. Drove me nuts."

"He have anything in that car?"

Finney held up his hands, as if saying, "Who remembers?"

"Think."

"Well . . . some books."

"What kind?"

"Schoolbooks."

"Remember the type of books?"

"Yeah, I guess. I think one said chemistry. I took chemistry."

"The others?"

Finney relaxed for a moment, as if to ponder, to remember back. "I think they were all that."

"Chemistry?"

"Yeah. But it's tough to remember."

Then Karlov recalled something else Finney had said. "You mentioned the pictures of kids. You sure they were *his* kids?"

"He said they were."

"How old?"

"Oh, young kids. Maybe six, seven, a little younger. One boy, one girl."

Then Karlov backed off and began to pace. He sensed he'd hit on something, one of those little bits of a puzzle that comes out through this kind of questioning. If Howe's kids were that young, what were chemistry books doing in the car? Was Howe involved in chemistry? Was he a teacher? Or was his wife? By now Karlov had a full report from Chicago police on the original arrest of Everett Morton Howe, and had a fairly clear picture of his early life. He'd been a quiet kid, but not entirely a loner. Some had thought him a little odd, but nothing more. He'd been an engineering student at the University of Illinois when arrested, and campus newspapers of the time reported his professors as stunned.

Engineering. Maybe that was the key word. An engineering student might also go on to study chemistry. Who knew what Howe had been up to since his escape from the mental hospital in 1977? Maybe he'd become a scientist, maybe a pillar of some community. Maybe he'd completely changed and was leading a crime-free life. Or maybe he was the man who'd stalked and murdered three women in their apartments in Manhattan.

"He say what he did for a living?" Karlov asked the young patrolman.

"I really don't remember," Finney replied.

"Well, did he have anything to indicate a company, an ID card, a sticker on the car?"

Finney dropped his head. "I really didn't notice, sir. I was new at this. Y'know, you sometimes don't remember everything they teach you."

"Yeah," Karlov agreed. "I know. But tell me, how was he dressed? Rich guy? Poor guy?"

"That I remember," Finney answered. "He had sort of a sport jacket. Not very expensive."

Karlov ended the interview and went to work. The

chemistry angle still intrigued him—a man with young children with chemistry books in his car. A man interested in science. A scientist would have to be meticulous, work with precision, give attention to detail. A pattern was emerging that suggested Karlov *might* be tracking the right man. He decided to pursue the chemistry connection by contacting every high school, college, science lab and technical corporation in the New York area, sending them pictures of Howe last taken when he was still in a mental hospital. Although Howe was using a false name and license plates, Karlov guessed he might well be living in or near Fair Lawn, New Jersey, as he had claimed, using the false documents in tight situations, as when Finney had stopped him.

*　　*　　*

Six days after interviewing the young patrolman, Karlov found himself in the office of the president of Kern International, a pharmaceutical supply exporter in Fair Lawn, New Jersey. Kern had one of those brick, one-story headquarters that dotted the New Jersey landscape just off the Garden State Parkway. It was only six years old, but already had opened offices in three European countries. It was a "hot" company that had linked up with several suppliers to export hard-to-manufacture drugs, some of which had been developed for the space program. Its president, Fernando Martinez, had a PhD in chemistry from Harvard, was the son of a Mexican university president, yet spoke and acted like Lee Iacocca. Heavy-set, with wide, expressive eyes, he puffed on his cigar as he sat behind a six-foot-wide glass desk in an office cushioned with inch-high red pile carpeting. Leonard Karlov sat opposite, in a high-backed leather visitors' chair that extended well above the top of his head, making him feel that he was sitting either on a throne or on the electric chair. He had the feeling the latter was what Martinez preferred, for this was clearly the chair in which subordinates sat to be chewed out.

Martinez spoke with only a touch of a Spanish accent. The only thing Spanish in the entire office, indeed the entire building, was a hand-carved Peruvian pistol on his desk, mounted on an oak stand and pointed directly at the visitor's chair. Karlov had seen tough in his career, but this was tough chic, the kind of thing a Texas store might sell in a Christmas catalogue.

"Yeah, I hired the guy in your picture," Martinez was saying. "Liked him. Smart guy. Smart. Liked his thinking. Had a BA in chem from some city college in Boston. I don't remember. Who the goddam hell cares? I like guys like that. Didn't go to the fancy schools like me. They think from the street. But he knew chem. Knew it. Had ideas for export. Good mind. Liked to tinker with things, like me. Once saw him repair the computer in his office. Took him twenty minutes."

"May I ask, sir," Karlov interrupted, a bit thrown by the atmosphere and the billowing cigar smoke enveloping his head, "what he did here?"

"Account executive. Complex drugs. Had to know some chem. Had to know it. You like my pistol?"

"Yes."

"Yeah, a cop would like it. He handled some foreign accounts."

"Did he have references?"

"Never depend on references, m'man. They're all baloney. I mean, who ever brings a bad reference?"

"Did he account for all his years?"

"No. Why should he? Said he had some jobs, then decided to go back to school late in life. Admire that. Guy had drive. Did college up there in three years. Older guys are serious."

"So you knew nothing of his earlier life?"

"What was I, writing his biography? A man has a right to drift. I drifted. Went to Harvard when I was twenty-seven. If a man can do the job, and works weekends, I don't care if he was Jack the Ripper." For the first time, Martinez paused. "Maybe I shouldn't say that. I mean, you're here for this guy. Did he—?"

"There may be a problem," Karlov answered.

"What kind?"

"I'd rather not say. Department policy."

"Oh, Yeah. Can't disagree. Right of privacy. That's what makes this country great. Is this missing persons?"

"Well, it could be. He *is* missing."

"Yeah, he sure is. One day, November 1984 it was, he just called up and said he wasn't coming in. Quit on the phone. Personal reasons. Never saw him again."

"Did you suspect anything?"

"No. His accounts were in order. Never stole anything. I guess sometimes a man wants to wander. He had no obligations."

"No family?"

"No. Not that I know of. Lived in an apartment—I told you his name was Kreiger."

"False name."

"Well, so be it. I knew him as Kreiger. Never mentioned a family. My personnel people tell me he paid his rent, couple months for breaking his lease, then just left. No forwarding address."

Karlov realized why Howe had behaved so strangely. November 1984 was when he was stopped by Finney. He might have become frightened, fearful that Finney would remember his face. It was clear he'd decided to disappear for a while. He may well have used several aliases and moved around often—a classic pattern, the escapee trying to hide, to melt in, to watch for any sign that he was being trailed. But if Howe *were* the killer of the three girls, he'd probably remained in the New York area, changing his appearance and getting a job as far away from chemistry as he could.

"Can I help?" Martinez asked. "Look, I'm not a detective, but I'm a citizen. I'll be straight. I don't want this guy's name linked to the business. We're clean here. I mean, we deal in drugs. Legitimate drugs. But people hear drugs, then hear a criminal worked here."

"We'd never embarrass you," Karlov assured him.

"My Spanish name won't help. I may need a lawyer on this one. Hate lawyers. All they do is talk and charge."

"I've heard."

"You need anything more from me?"

"Just one thing," Karlov replied. "Did this man ever do anything suspicious?"

"No. Sterling employee. Frankly, I'd like him back if he was on the level."

*   *   *

Karlov left Martinez, believing the trail had run cold. Howe was smart. He was constantly conscious of being caught. He might even decide to stop killing and go to a different state, maybe even a different country. Karlov drove back to New York discouraged. The papers were crying for action; even the mayor had expressed concern over the pace of the investigation. Women's groups were becoming active, one even charging that the police department was indifferent because all the victims had been women.

Everett Morton Howe was Karlov's only name, his only lead. He knew that dogged police work like this, tracking down every lead step by step, was the way virtually all criminals were caught. But he also knew that Howe, no matter how well he fit the profile of the serial murderer, might not be his man at all, might even be dead, that all this work might be for nothing.

The murderer of Constance Rainey, Deborah Moore and Marie Gould simply didn't leave a trail. He was an artist in his speciality.

Karlov had a strange respect for him, a respect tinged with fear, for maybe this man was the perfect criminal committing the perfect crimes.

Maybe he was uncatchable.

11

The repairman drove the red Ford through the Queens-Midtown Tunnel into Manhattan, blasting the air conditioner and listening to WCBS, always on the alert for some report on Karlov's investigation. Tonight there was none. Leonard Karlov had nothing say, nothing to reveal. Women were simply told to be cautious about whom they let in. And, typical of the New York approach to crime, WCBS ran a symposium of psychiatrists discussing the psychiatric effects on women, and even on young girls, of the constant headlines about the murders. New York, with the most psychoanalyzed population in the world, lives on paranoia, dishing it out between commericials for travel agencies and condominiums.

The repairman hit a traffic jam because of an accident on West Thirty-fourth Street, but drove around it and toward the Upper West Side. He'd already called ahead to confirm his appointment, one he'd looked forward to for weeks.

He hit Columbus Avenue, not long ago a declining street—empty at night, depressing in the day. Now it jumped, fueled by the gentrification of the West Side and an almost uncountable number of restaurants and boutiques. He liked the crowds on the sidewalk. Crowds gave him a sense of security, of being unnoticed by those who had more important things to stare at. He glanced down at the seat beside him where the name and address of his intended were written. Carol Krindler lived on West Eighty-eighth Street in an old building that had become a cooperative only six months before. The repairman had studied the building, passed it at night and during the day. He was satisfied.

He knew Carol Krindler was a photographer for an architecture magazine. He knew that she had job offers in San Francisco, which she loved, and that she wanted to pursue them. He knew her father was seriously ill.

He knew so much about her. He was proud of the amount of information he had on his subjects, proud of the methods he had developed for getting all the facts he needed. Most of all, he was proud that he was standing up for himself. His father never thought he'd stand up. Those kids back home, they'd never thought so either. But he was standing up.

He parked on West Ninetieth Street and got out, carrying his little box of tools inside a new shoulder bag. He bent down outside the car to check himself in a side-view mirror—the glasses, the hair, the muted sport shirt. Amazing, he thought, what a few changes could do. Then he glanced around and saw that some old woman was watching from a window, and he started walking.

Now, that may have been a mistake, he thought. People usually don't check themselves in outside car mirrors. He chastised himself, and silently pledged that he would never make a mistake like that again.

As he approached West Eighty-eighth Street, his pace quickened and his heart began to pound. It was always this way, the normal reactions of a man going to what he dreamed was a romantic encounter.

But, suddenly, his ears rang with a piercing, screaming sound.

At first, echoing off the buildings, it resembled a shriek.

Then, it was clearer. A siren.

More than one. *Sirens. Many* sirens.

The repairman whipped around, looking for some conflagration, some medical emergency on the street. He saw none, convincing himself that the sirens were heading in some other direction.

But they weren't.

The sirens grew closer. They were heading for *him*.

It was only twenty seconds later when he saw the first of the police cars, lights flashing, passenger door half open as an officer waited to jump out, Hollywood style.

His mind raced. What was the right strategy?

Stop, he told himself.

The least suspicious thing was to stop, and at least look. No one would ever suspect a man who stopped.

Now, three more cars pulled up. Uniformed cops got out, guns drawn.

Hell. He hadn't planned on this kind of party. What was going on? A murder? Someone stealing his thunder?

Or . . . no.

No, it couldn't be. They couldn't be coming for *him*. They couldn't have been tipped off. No one else knew. This was *his* secret, his plan. But maybe they'd picked something up, some clue he'd overlooked. Maybe they'd followed him. Or maybe Carol Krindler began to suspect, and called the police.

He stood still, fighting to prevent fear from wiping over his face. He rubbed his right ear again and again.

But then the horde of cops whizzed past him, thrusting a warm wind his way. They piled into a brownstone where only a single light burned. One cop, obviously a rookie, obviously confused about just what to do, waited on the sidewalk to keep bystanders back.

The repairman suddenly heard the voices from the brownstone. One man. One woman. And cops. The screaming and cursing cut the night air, audible even over the honking horns from Broadway and Amsterdam Avenue.

The repairman did the least suspicious thing—he sauntered over to the rookie to ask the logical question.

"What happened?"

The rookie shrugged, then smiled, not yet having learned that an experienced cop never smiles at a crime scene. "Domestic," he replied.

"Domestic?" the repairman asked.

"Family dispute. Some guy hit his wife."

"Oh, yeah," the repairman said. "Figures. Hot weather."

The repairman turned away and started down the block once more, musing how he had thought himself in danger, and how he had come face to face with a member of a police department that was desperately searching for him.

He walked to West Eighty-eighth Street and pulled open the heavy glass outer door of Carol Krindler's building. He had to restrict his operations to this type of building, for a doorman would be too strong a witness. He walked over to the intercom and pressed the small black button next to the card that said KRINDLER 8D. Then he waited.

It was a long time. Much longer than the others. But, finally, Carol Krindler answered.

"Zenith," the repairman said.

He heard the buzzer that unlocked the inner door, and entered the lobby. Just then the elevator opened and a gray-haired man in a suit walked out, accompanied by a tiny white-haired woman. The repairman tried to avoid eye contact, but for a flash it was there. That man's eyes stared at him, stared at him with a kind of hostility born of experience.

"Want something?" the man asked, with a strong European accent.

"Visiting," the repairman replied.

"Who?"

The repairman hesitated. He didn't know any other names in the building. That was a mistake. He should have memorized one or two names from the list on the intercom. "My cousin," he replied.

"Who's your cousin?" the man demanded to know. It was the European background, the repairman sensed. He'd seen a lot in his younger days. The man was suspicious, fearful, frightened of strange faces.

"Carol Krindler," the repairman replied. He thought fast. He thought ahead. That was the right answer, the *unsuspicious* answer.

"Oh, Carol," the man said, as his wife began tugging at his arm, urging him on. "A nice girl. Find her a boy."

"Come on, Seymour," the wife said, and pulled him along.

"I will," the repairman answered, and entered the elevator. It hadn't been a very smooth night. Little things had gone wrong, but this was a *big* thing. If he had to kill again, those two old people would come forward. They were the type. The solid citizen type. They'd be able to describe him and say that he carried a shoulder bag, that he wore glasses and said he was Carol Krindler's cousin. And then the police would have to decide if *he* was the one they were looking for, or just one of several visitors that night. And they would investigate and find that Carol Krindler had no cousin fitting that description, and that he was either the murderer or some other visitor saying he was a cousin out of embarrassment.

And yet, had he made up the name of the person he was visiting, that gray-haired man would have known. He was the kind to know everyone in the building, their apartment numbers, their backgrounds and problems. Now the repairman had to make a choice—go up to Carol Krindler and take the risk, or run. To run, he knew, would arouse its own suspicion. After all, he'd already called up. He'd identified himself and used the Zenith name. If he failed to show, Carol Krindler might call Zenith to complain, and that would open up endless possibilities.

But there was another choice. He could return to the lobby and call up once more, saying he'd discovered he didn't have the right part with him. He could apologize and say he'd call for another appointment. But what would happen when he didn't call? Would Krindler forget? Or would she call Zenith in *that* situation as well, complaining about the repairman who'd kept her home, then didn't show, then didn't call?

The elevator reached Carol Krindler's floor. The door opened. The repairman pressed a button to keep it open while he decided.

He decided to go ahead.

Appearances could be changed. If his appearance were described to the police, he'd simply do something about the glasses, and get some other bag for his tools and the little gondola. And he knew, for he had studied the history of serial murderers, that there was a better than even chance that the old man and his wife would get the description wrong, or disagree.

No, better to take the chance. Arousing Krindler's suspicions was worse.

He rang her doorbell. He felt the heat churning up inside him.

Having buzzed him up, she opened the door without even asking who it was.

*   *   *

She stood there in a sheer summer dress, long blond hair flowing down below her shoulders, the slightest touch of dampness on her brow.

"I hope you can look at my refrigerator, too," she said, with a touch of a Southwestern accent. "It's not a Zenith, but . . ."

"Sure," the repairman replied as he entered. "I've worked on refrigerators. Why don't I take care of the TV first?"

"Okay. It's in my bedroom. It used to be in here, but y'know, I always found I wanted to watch it in bed."

"Naturally," the repairman said. He always liked it when the TV was in the bedroom. It was the right atmosphere.

"My father once sued a TV company," Carol Krindler went on. "The set broke the first night and they refused to fix it. My father's tough. He won. They had to give him a new set and pay his legal expenses."

"Terrific," the repairman said. "We don't like those companies that give us a bad name."

He smiled at Carol, but he noticed she was staring at him, especially as they entered the light blue bedroom, which was better lit than the entrance hall.

She kept staring at him as he walked toward the TV. A questioning look came over her face.

He hadn't seen that in his subjects before. Then her eyes narrowed.

"Something wrong?" he asked.

"No," she replied. "But—"

"But what?"

"*Aren't you . . . ?*"

Carol Krindler had been something of a heavy-weight—her father was a major Texas lawyer with connections on Wall Street. The heat was turned on the New York Police Department.

But one item didn't appear in the papers. There was no description of the killer, no report of anyone seeing him at all. The man who'd quizzed him in the lobby and his wife were simply too frightened to come forward. Now that they knew the man they'd questioned was a multiple killer, they cowered in their apartment, hoping he didn't remember them. They were beaten by the fear that has enveloped large cities.

*   *   *

Leonard Karlov inspected Carol Krindler's one-bedroom apartment, as if the inspection had become a kind of ritual. Once again there was the little gondola at the victim's head.

75

Once again there was no sign of struggle. But there were two differences that fascinated him, differences that he could not immediately explain. In the three other murders, the victims had surprised expressions on their faces. This victim's face was simply contorted, as if she had begun to resist. And the fatal wound was in the *back*. Perhaps she turned to run. Perhaps he had grabbed her.

Karlov never considered the possibility that Carol Krindler *suddenly recognized* her attacker. She had, after all, let him in, as had the others. Nothing made sense.

Harold Kramer arrived to examine the body. He and Karlov spoke, almost in whispers, in Carol Krindler's bedroom, decorated with pictures of Texas horses and a painting of cowboys.

"Len," Kramer said, "this one was different. The wound was ragged, not smooth."

"Sudden attack?" Karlov asked.

"I think so. Or he didn't expect to attack her when he did. Maybe he *had* to. Maybe he ran into some kind of trouble he didn't have before."

Karlov noted also that there was no sign of any relaxed conversation before the murder. There'd been soft drinks left out the other times. Here there was nothing. And some papers on a small table near the door were scattered widely, as if the killer had made a fast escape.

* * *

Francine Connor, a five-foot-eleven fashion model, Carol Krindler's closest friend in New York, rushed to the apartment as soon as the news came through on radio. She tried to remain composed, even as she stared at the covered body of the young woman she had seen just an hour before the repairman arrived. Dressed in khaki, with a narrow leather belt at the waist, and large sunglasses that hid a good part of her smallish face, she sat down with Karlov and Kramer in the bedroom to answer a few questions about her friend. Her hands trembled, her skin seemed to tighten. She, too, was from Texas. That was what had brought the women together, although they'd never known each other at home. Despite her best efforts, her voice cracked as she spoke to the two men, and small town drowned out big city. She'd become so used to striking a pose, creating an image, that she was at odds when real feelings began to flow.

"We were close, we sure were," she told Karlov, looking down at the throw rugs that dotted the bedroom. "I spoke to her last night. I live three blocks from here."

"Did she mention that anyone else was coming, ma'am?" Karlov asked.

"No."

"No dates?"

"No. Carol was kinda shy. Yeah, she sure was shy. She didn't have too many what you call dates. She knew a lot of guys from photography, but when the day was done she liked to close up, if you know what I mean."

"Maybe there was someone professional visiting her."

Francine Connor shrugged. Karlov noticed how skin-and-bones her shoulders were. "If anyone was coming over, it'd be on the chalk board," she said.

"What chalk board?" Karlov asked urgently.

"You didn't find it?"

"No."

Francine got up slowly and sauntered across the bedroom to a white formica wall unit with a number of drawers and cabinets. She pointed to one cabinet, below her eye level. "On the other side of this door is a little chalk board.

Carol never kept a calendar, or anything like that. When she had an appointment she wrote it on that board. Shall I turn it around? I don't want to touch anything.''

"Turn it around," Karlov told her.

Francine's long, graceful hand reached out to the cabinet door. She opened it, then pushed it open all the way, so its inside was turned out. "I don't believe this," she said, glancing at an absolutely blank piece of wood.

"Could she have put it somewhere else?" Kramer asked.

"No, it was always here."

Karlov ordered the police team still lingering in the living room to search the apartment for the board. Perhaps it had been missed on the earlier search. But the new search turned up nothing.

*   *   *

Karlov came up with an explanation. In all the other murders, he had been baffled at not finding an appointment calendar. Young, professional women surely kept appointment calendars. He'd assumed that the murderer had searched for the calendars and had taken them. It fit in with the theory that he was incredibly meticulous. A less careful killer would simply have ripped out the page listing his appointment with the victim, but this man knew that anything written leaves impressions underneath, so taking the entire calendar made sense.

The same was probably true of the chalk board, Karlov thought. The killer could simply have erased the board with a cloth. But perhaps he feared the chalk markings left some kind of impression in the board, and so he took the whole thing. He was never in too much of a rush to search for and eliminate any incriminating evidence.

After he realized they were not going to find the board,

Karlov returned to his questioning of Francine Connor, who'd waited patiently.

"Do you know of any threats Carol received?" Karlov asked.

"No, I don't," Francine replied.

"Was Carol involved in any unusual activity?"

"No. She had her photo assignments, but they were routine. She was looking for things in other cities..."

"Why?"

"Opportunities. She thought she'd go further."

"She planned to move?"

"Yeah, if she got something. I mean, she told me how expensive it was to live in San Francisco, although less than New York."

"So she wanted to go there?"

"Well, even though we were close, she didn't tell me everything. But I think she was pretty determined. She had the apartment for sale recently, then took it off. Y'know, testing the waters."

* * *

Karlov wrote it all down, then asked Francine for the standard list of Carol's friends. Within twenty-four hours Karlov asked the same questions of others who knew Carol Krindler, including her closest relatives in Texas. But, although there were slight differences between this and the other murders, the bottom line was the same. No names appeared on Carol Krindler's lists that appeared on any of the others.

* * *

Again, Karlov turned to a little gondola, this one placed at the head of Carol Krindler. He still found it hard to believe that the careful, scientific killer had overlooked the fact that the gondolas could be melted down. Maybe he'd bought them, Karlov reasoned. Or maybe he didn't realize they'd been made from newspapers. Or maybe he was trying to tell the police something.

13

At Twentieth Precinct headquarters, while a summer rainstorm came down in torrents outside, Karlov started peeling down the gondola. Harold Kramer watched as Karlov went through the operation that had earlier revealed the Chicago connection. The little bathroom was stifling, the pipe underneath the sink dripping cold water onto the grimy tile floor. A policeman who'd used the facility earlier had taped up a poster for an upcoming march against a district attorney "soft on crime," scrawling on the bottom, "Be there!"

Bit by bit, the strips of paper that made up the outer shell of the gondola melted away and dropped, with little plopping sounds, into the sink. Karlov carefully examined each one. And, with each one, came disappointment. They were from the same Chicago newspapers he'd seen previously. "Nothing," he told Kramer, impatience in his voice. "The same stuff. How many corpses do we have to have before we get something?''

But he pushed on, stripping the gondola down further, almost exposing its wire frame. Suddenly, something caught his eye: a different type style, a different column width. He waited expectantly until the strip finally sagged, buckled, then fell.

Carefully, he picked it up.

''We've got it,'' he whispered.

Kramer rushed forward.

''Winnetka, Illinois,'' Karlov said.

''You sure?''

''The paper is a local Winnetka paper.''

''That doesn't mean he came from there.''

''Hal, these little-town papers don't travel far.''

But there were more strips on the gondola's frame. One was from the *Chicago Tribune*. It contributed nothing. But another was from the same Winnetka paper, dated June 1964. Karlov picked it up, almost caressed it in his hand as he read each word. There were bits of stories, one about a wedding, one about a flower show. But there were letters— an odd grouping of letters—at the ragged corner of one strip.

ezia.

''What the hell is this?'' he asked Kramer.

Kramer stood next to Karlov and glanced down at the strip. ''I wasn't good in language,'' Kramer replied, his heavy breath creating a small circle of fog in the bathroom's stained mirror. ''*Ezia.* I don't know.''

Karlov seemed to contemplate for a moment. ''Maybe it's Italian or Spanish.''

''So?''

''Italian or Spanish. I mean, I know enough about language for that. My father spoke a little Italian.''

"So?"

"The gondolas," Karlov replied, "are from Italy. At least the real ones are. This is an Italian word in a Winnetka, Illinois, paper. Why?"

Kramer looked down. *"Venezia,"* he said softly.

Karlov stared at him. "Venice," he replied, "in Italian."

14

"**O**f course it shakes me up," Laura Barnett said, as she paced her living room nervously. Glen was watching her, trying to console her, trying to make her feel safe. On a table was the Post's banner headline, TEXAS HEIRESS LATEST VICTIM, with a small picture of Carol Krindler, and another of her prominent Texas father.

Laura stopped to stare at the headline, but that was not the cause of her crisis. Next to the newspaper, still partially wrapped, was a bottle of champagne, sent through ordinary Parcel Post with a small note enclosed: *For the good times we'll have*. The note was printed in green Magic Marker.

"It's him," Laura finally said, as if she'd been trying to deny the obvious authorship of the note and source of the champagne. "I know his style."

"Come on," Glen said, "you can't be sure. It's like the candy. It could be some joke. I tell you, it could even be a friend of *mine*. You know, someone hears that two people get together, and the pranks begin.''

Laura turned to Glen, who was immaculate in a lawyer's pin-striped suit, complete with vest. For the first time since they'd met, he saw her bright blue eyes glazed over.

She was anguished, fearful that something was happening that she'd *known* would happen. ''Glen,'' she said, ''I want to tell you something.''

''Tell me.''

''When Jason left for the last time...he raised his hands above his head as if making some solemn pledge to God. He said he'd be back. He meant it, Glen. I've always known he meant it.''

Glen was silent for a few moments. He'd always quipped that the year and a half he'd spent in the U.S. attorney's office might come in handy some day. This was the day. ''You're convinced it wasn't an idle threat?'' he asked.

''I'm convinced.''

''Yet you stayed here, sweet. If you thought he'd be back...''

Laura sighed, finally collapsing in a chair, worn down by the reality of what was happening. ''I'd always handled him,'' she said. ''I handled his crazy moods, his shouting, his artistic passions. I guess I denied to myself that he was dangerous. I guess I thought that if he came back, I'd handle it again. But...these gifts...I mean, if he'd just call. But this gives me the creeps.''

''Then we've got a problem,'' Glen conceded. Now he started pacing.

''What do we do?''

Laura realized that this was their first serious crisis. Everything up to now had been a kind of make-believe that made life wonderful but blotted out reality. She had full confidence in Glen, but realized she'd never seen him actually deal with a problem.

"We start with evidence," Glen said.

"What about it?"

"We haven't got any."

"The candy, the champagne . . ." Laura said.

"We'd have to prove they came from Jason. He may have his fingerprints on them, but maybe not. People see so many crime shows, they know to wipe them off. Also, the printing on that note looks like it was written in such a way that no one could trace it."

"All right," Laura said, "what if there *are* prints and we *can* trace them, and they're Jason's."

"Then we have another problem," Glen answered. Now he folded his arms, thinking carefully. "Jason isn't doing anything illegal."

"But I don't want his presents."

"Then you have a right to refuse them. Next time you get a box with no return address, refuse it."

"What if they keep coming?"

"Continue to refuse. He might get the message."

"Glen, darling," Laura explained, "you don't know this man. Besides, with no return address, the boxes won't go back to him. They'll wind up in the post office, right?"

"Sure."

"So he'll never know they were refused."

"Of course, but you'll be doing nothing to respond to him either. One of the boxes might include a note, asking you to call him. Or, he might start using return addresses. He might identify himself."

But Glen knew the issue wasn't simply legalistic. Laura was living in fear. "If we *could* prove it's Jason," he went on, "I might be able to charge harassment, or implied use of the mails to coerce. Something like that. I never worked postal cases. But in the absence of a crime, it would be tough. He has no police record, does he?''

''Not that I know of.''

''My biggest concern isn't the packages,'' Glen said. ''It's the chance that he—''

''Go on.'' They were both thinking the same thing.

''That he might appear here. If he's what you say, he could have gotten worse.''

Suddenly the reality of a physical threat was before them, one that could strike at any time.

''Glen,'' Laura said, her tone almost pleading, ''there must be *something* the police can do.''

''Do you know how many complaints the police get every day?'' Glen asked.

''No,'' she said sadly.

''Too many. And especially too many when there's no crime involved. Look at it from their point of view: Laura Barnett comes in and says she's getting presents from an old boyfriend, an artist. Laura Barnett is scared. They ask, 'Did the boyfriend ever assault you?' Laura Barnett says, 'No, Sergeant.' They ask, 'Did he ever pull a weapon on you?' Laura Barnett replies, 'No, Sergeant . . .' ''

''I'm getting the picture,'' Laura sighed. ''So you don't want to go to the police at all?''

''Didn't say that,'' Glen replied. ''I think you should file a report. I can call an old friend in the U.S. attorney's office and see if we can get a detective to question Jason.''

''Can they do that—legally?''

''Sure. It might put a scare into him. In the meantime—'' He stopped. He knew he was about to raise a point that was sensitive with Laura because of a family background she always called ''traditional.''

''Go on,'' she urged him.

''In the meantime, maybe I'd better move in.''

Laura didn't answer for a time. She knew Glen was thinking of her personal safety. He had always been respectful of her personal wishes, her desire for that "traditional" courtship. She fidgeted with a ring on her right hand, then brushed some dust from her dark blue Italian linen skirt. "I'd have trouble with that one," she finally said.

"But I could watch out for you," Glen told her.

"I know. But look, I don't open the door to anyone. And Jason's not the type to run up and attack me with a cleaver. He'd try to get in and convince me. If he failed, and he would . . . that's when I'd worry. But I'm not really afraid to stay alone. He'd just never get in here."

Glen looked at her skeptically. "I'd hate to lose you," he said. His mind immediately flashed to the victims of the serial murderer who had terrorized the neighborhood. Some man didn't want to lose *those* women either.

"You won't lose me," Laura assured him as he went to her and took her in his arms, holding her tightly.

But what if he did? The thought churned over and over in Laura's mind, even as she felt his masculine warmth. What would his life be like? Was it fair to *him* to take any risks at all? Maybe they should live together. Maybe she should violate her attachment to the old decorum. She owed him so much—her current happiness, their future life together. Maybe he was right.

She came to no conclusion as he nudged her toward the bedroom. Laura dreaded living with fear. It was unfair. It was wrong.

Why couldn't Jason just go *away*.

15

Jim Hurley waited in a worn-out rocker for Karlov's call. He knew it would come any day. It *had* to. Karlov would depend on him, just as other detectives had depended on him in the good old days. He was ready for action, prepared to go into the blazing Chicago sun for Len Karlov, to restore himself, to do an honest job.

But when the phone rang—and it rarely rang in the Hurley household—he waited. Never answer a phone on the first ring. It *might* be someone important, and you never want to look too anxious. He waited for the third ring, and picked up.

"Hurley."

"Jim, Len Karlov."

"Why, Len, what a surprise."

"Just calling to bother you again on this serial murder," Karlov said.

"Read you had another one." Hurley hadn't only read

about it, he'd clipped every article he could, just to be ready for Karlov.

"A bad one," Karlov confirmed. "Jim, there was another one of these little boats. One of the newspapers inside came from Winnetka."

"North of Chicago," Hurley said.

"Yeah, Jim, I know. I looked it up in the atlas. I also know it's near Skokie, where our friend Howe grew up."

"True," Hurley said. "A Jewish town, Skokie." Then he hesitated, realizing that the observation was the kind that respectable people no longer made. He feared for a moment that Karlov . . . he didn't know his background. "Not that it matters, Len. Respected people."

"Sure, Jim. I understand. Look, we found a word on one of the papers. We figured it out as *Venezia,* the Italian word for Venice."

"With the little boats," Hurley interjected.

"Right. Maybe there's a connection, Jim. Maybe something was going on in Winnetka about Venice that June in 1964, something that might give us a shove."

"Could be," Hurley answered. He began taking notes with a plain yellow pencil and some scrap paper. "Want me to check it?"

"Could you, Jim? I know it's outside your jurisdiction . . ."

"Former jurisdiction," Hurley sighed. He had this kind of death wish, this insistence on always bringing up his forced separation from the department.

"Whatever," Karlov said, not wanting to extend the awkward moment. "Maybe you know people up there."

" 'Course I know them. I went to many parades up there, Len. We'd send contingents."

"I need help," Karlov said.

16

It was maddening for Karlov. The failed leads, the sense that he *might* know the serial killer's name and yet couldn't get to him, the sure knowledge that other women would die, the nagging fear that he'd overlooked something. He knew that each piece of information drew him closer to a solution and narrowed the potential suspects. But, as he'd often told students in lectures at the police academy, narrowing the suspects in a nation of 230 million did not merit the Medal of Honor.

The phone on his desk rang. It was an anemic, hesitant ring typical of old equipment, yet it pierced Karlov's ears like a scream in the Siberian night. He glanced at the phone, wondering what bad news it would bring. He answered.

"Karlov."

There was some static at the other end, but, after a delay of a few seconds, a voice. "Len?"

Jim Hurley. "Yes," Karlov replied, his voice beginning to crack.

"Len, this is Jim Hurley."

"I know, Jim." Karlov could sense the excitement in Hurley's voice, the excitement of vindication.

"Len, I'm in Winnetka. Calling from a shopping center. I've got it for you."

"What've you got?"

"*Venezia.*"

"Let's have it." Karlov's heart raced.

"You're right about the town, Len," Hurley answered, sweat forming on his brow inside the blazing phone booth. "In June, nineteen and sixty-four, the high school here had their senior prom. The label on it—"

"The theme?"

"Yeah, Len, the theme . . . was *Venezia.*"

"Terrific," Karlov said softly. He wasn't sure quite how terrific it was. Maybe it meant nothing. But pieces were linking together, and he'd never known that to be bad.

"Now, that's not all," Hurley continued. "I checked what happened at the prom, seein' as you had these little boats."

"Gondolas."

"Yeah. So I checked. They had a whole bunch of 'em at this here prom. But a funny thing . . . they got swiped right after."

"They ever find out who?"

"Nope. They guessed it was some kind of joke— maybe kids from another school. They was supposed to be cleaned up, taken away, the next mornin'. But when the kids came in, they was gone."

"Jim, did anyone find a trace of 'em?"

"Nope. I talked to people at the school who remembered. Never a trace. But no one thought much of it—just little boats some kids made for decorations. Boy, it's hot in here.''

"Sorry, Jim. You in a booth?"

"Yeah."

"Look, go get some air. You've done great work. I appreciate it. This *will* help us . . . and you'll get the credit."

"Thanks," Hurley replied in a whisper. The two men ended their conversation, Hurley left the phone booth, leaned against it, and cried like a baby.

* * *

Karlov jotted a summary of what he had. The gondolas had been from a prom in 1964 in Winnetka, Illinois. They'd been stolen afterward; now they'd been found at the heads of murder victims, none of whom apparently had any connection with Winnetka.

Questions began flowing through Karlov's mind. Why would anyone keep the gondolas for more than two decades? Were they used in the murders because they *meant* something, or were they just convenient markers? Why were they all pointing in one direction—the direction, Karlov now realized, of Winnetka, Illinois? If Everett Howe was indeed the man, what connection did he have to that Winnetka prom?

Karlov had to track down people who knew something about the 1964 prom and find out if anything had happened there that would give him a clue to four murders more than twenty years later. These people were now in their late thirties. Most were married, with or without children, some probably divorced, maybe a few dead. Karlov knew that he might well wind up phoning the murderer himself if it were someone other than Everett Howe. He, Karlov, might well tip the killer that the police were closing in. It was a dismal thought, a thought that gave him momentary pause. It was a risk, he realized, he'd have to take, or the investigation would stop in place.

It took several calls to Winnetka school authorities before Karlov got the name of the person he thought would prove most helpful in the next stage—the president of the alumni class of 1964. Like many from the Chicago area, she'd drifted east. She had attended Middlebury College, then married a stockbroker and moved to Long Island.

17

It was a humid day with light, ground-hugging fog when Karlov took the traffic-stalled Long Island Expressway to Great Neck. Although he'd grown up in New York, he'd never been to Great Neck before, not even to the towns surrounding it. Great Neck had an intimidating ring to it, an image of affluence, of success, of a town off limits to the civil service and certainly to the modestly educated son of Russian immigrants, especially if that son carried a New York City badge. Great Neck, in his imagination, was a town where the only sound one heard was the breeze rustling through the trees.

But as he drove his Chevrolet up Middle Neck Road through the center of town, he encountered a small metropolis, with street after street of stores, and traffic to rival the best of Broadway at five P.M. It was not until he battled through the business district that he made the right turn into Kensington and saw the Great Neck of his own imagination—

large, traditional houses, most built before World War II, each with a lawn whose edges were as straight as the creases on a Marine's trousers. He found his way to Arleigh Road, pulling into the driveway of a colonial with a Buick Electra in the garage. He got out, heard the poodle barking at him from the front door, took a small folder from the passenger seat and walked slowly up the flagstone path, feeling a serenity that would have been impossible in the city.

He rang the doorbell, fully expecting that it would be answered by a maid wearing an apron and holding a skillet. Instead, Deborah Stone came to the door, Mrs. Warren Stone, avid worker for charity, child of the Kennedy era, yet someone who wore the appropriate badges of success—an obviously expensive green linen dress and a Rolex gold-and-steel watch. She was slim, almost too much so, rather small, with a tan that showed off her afternoons at the golf course.

Routinely, Karlov pulled his badge from his gray, eighty-nine-dollar Bond suit. "Karlov, NYPD, ma'am," he said. "Are you Mrs. Stone?"

"I am," Deborah Stone replied with a smile, standing aside for Karlov to enter. She was remarkably relaxed for someone receiving a visit from the police, Karlov thought. Most people were tense, suspicious, fearful of authority. Deborah Stone had that perfect poise of someone who'd spent her entire adult life developing it.

Inside, though, her stomach was churning. She was sure Karlov had come about one of her neighbors, perhaps someone involved in a dubious financial scheme. It went with the territory—affluent towns attracted a certain number of people whose wealth didn't come from hard work and long nights at the office.

Karlov walked in, conscious of the worn heels on his

shoes and the lack of starch in his shirt. Immediately he felt himself sink into the blue pile carpeting. "Lovely home," he commented.

"Thank you," Deborah answered, gesturing for Karlov to go into the living room. "Please sit down."

Karlov sat on a couch covered in Haitian cotton. Deborah sat opposite. "Would you like something to drink?" Deborah asked. "It's so hot out there."

"Uh, no thanks, ma'am," Karlov replied. "Actually I hold up pretty well."

"Okay. You're a . . . detective, I think you said?"

"Yes, a detective lieutenant. Please don't be frightened by the title. I just want to ask some questions."

"Is someone in trouble?"

"Possibly. Frankly, I'm hoping to *get* someone in trouble. It's a murder case, ma'am."

"Oh." That she didn't expect.

"It doesn't involve anyone around here."

"Who *does* it involve?"

Karlov hesitated, looking around at the floral displays and oversized potted plants that framed the room. He'd been debating whether to reveal the complete purpose of his visit. He decided against it. He saw no point in encouraging fear, or neighborhood gossip. "Ma'am," he said, "I'd prefer not to go into details, if you don't mind."

Deborah had no reaction. The whole thing seemed to her like something out of a novel. She crossed her legs, leaned back, and was ready to listen. Somehow the word *murder* had not sunk in fully. She didn't know anyone who'd been murdered. She didn't know anyone connected with a murder case. She'd never seen violence or felt it close to her. Somehow the idyllic mood of the suburbs on a balmy day seemed to soften the whole idea of murder.

"Ma'am," Karlov continued, "you graduated from high school in Winnetka in 1964, is that right?"

Deborah seemed startled. Why was *this* important, this oblique reference to age? "Yes," she replied.

"And you're president of your class alumni association?"

"That's right. How did you know?"

"The school told me."

"What does it matter?"

"That's what I'm here to find out, Mrs. Stone. Is it Mrs. or Ms.?"

"Mrs.," Deborah replied with an ironic little laugh. "I was never converted."

"Now Mrs. Stone, do you recall your senior prom?"

"My senior *prom*?" No one ever asked about senior proms anymore. Alumni associations, yes. But high school dances? She shrugged, almost embarrassed to go back that far. "Yes, I guess I remember it vaguely. I went."

"Do you recall the theme?"

"Sure. Venice."

"Venezia?"

"Yes. Now why is *this* important?"

"Ma'am, I really don't know *how* important it is. I won't know until we finish. If you could just be patient, you could be very helpful."

"Yes. Yes, of course I'll be helpful," Deborah said. Karlov had perfected his technique of getting a witness on his side years before. He rarely became hostile or raised his voice, except when talking with a hardened criminal. Karlov took the gentle approach, and always tried to show compassion.

It was strange, he now felt, sitting amidst the opulence, but he didn't resent Deborah Stone. He didn't resent the wealth, the possessions, the obvious life of ease. He knew many cops who loathed the rich and resented having to protect them, often at the risk of their own lives. But Karlov was neutral. He could never quite understand why he didn't share these resentments. He was, fundamentally, a man who lived for his work, whose world was investigation, a man who was probably lucky that he never married, for it was unlikely that he could sustain any life outside the precinct.

"Now Mrs. Stone, did anything unusual happen at Venezia?"

"Unusual?"

"Something out of line, like a fistfight or someone getting drunk, or some argument..."

Deborah Stone gazed at Karlov as if the detective were certifiable. "Mr. Karlov," she replied, showing the first sign of condescension, "do you know how long ago this was?"

"Yes, ma'am. But it's important."

"Well, I'll try to remember back. I do remember how the gym was decorated, with Italian flags and tables with Italian foods, snacks you know..."

"Sure."

"And they had a band with Beatles music. The Beatles were just coming to America. They had four guys in the band trying to act just like them. God, they were awful."

Karlov smiled awkwardly. He hadn't even gone to his senior prom.

"And we danced a lot. It was happy, but sad, too. You know, Kennedy had been shot a few months before, and I think that took a lot out of our senior year..."

"I can understand."

"The teachers were there. In those days you had to have chaperones. And we...all had a good time."

"No horseplay?"

"Well, there's always something—"

"Like what?" He pounced on it.

"The usual pranks. We had these little gondolas, like from Venice . . ."

"Oh?"

"A lot of the kids made them from wire and papier-mâché, and we put them all around the room, on all the tables. They were very nice. I know that the prom committee wanted to give them out the next day to people who'd really worked on the thing—the committee people. But they were gone."

"That's too bad," Karlov said, writing it down as if hearing it for the first time.

"Yes, it *was* too bad. I don't know what anyone would want with them."

"There were no suspects?"

Again, Deborah stared at Karlov incredulously. "Suspects? What do you think we had, a police investigation?" She immediately cupped her right hand to her mouth. "I'm sorry," she said. "I didn't mean it the way it sounded."

"I understand," Karlov replied.

"We just let it go," Deborah went on. "We thought maybe the gondolas would turn up in some practical joke, but they never did. God, I didn't think I'd remember all this."

"Did you or anyone else have any idea *who* could have taken them?" Karlov asked.

"No, not really. Some of the guys thought it was kids from another school. Y'know, we saw some fellas cruising by during the prom. They could've gotten in after we left."

"But why the gondolas?" Karlov asked.

"Who knows?" Now Deborah had a slightly angry look on her face. "This is crazy," she said. "I know you have your reasons, but little toy boats at *my* senior prom . . . not hot stuff."

Karlov didn't respond. He simply reached into the

inner pocket of his suit and pulled out a small brown envelope. Inside was a black-and-white photograph, the kind normally taken for high school yearbooks. "Ma'am," he asked, "is it possible this boy took those gondolas?" He reached over and gave the photo to Deborah.

She gazed at the picture, turning beet red.

"Do you know who this *is?*" she asked, her neck muscles quivering. "Do you *know?*"

"Do *you?*" Karlov asked.

"Ev Howe."

"You knew him?"

"Knew him? I once went *out* with him! Do you know what he did?"

"Yes I do, ma'am."

"He killed a girl. And *I* went out with him. The Skokie boys were supposed to be nice. He was, but . . ."

"But what?"

"Well, we know the real story."

"Could he have taken those little boats?"

Deborah was still shocked by the picture of a "friend" from school. "I don't know," she answered, now becoming frightened and defensive. "How *would* I know? Look, I know he escaped. I read it in the papers. Jesus, is this about *him?*"

"It might be, Mrs. Stone. We're not sure." Karlov's voice still hadn't changed its tone.

"You know, I'm a little scared," Deborah said.

"No reason to be. Did he have anything *against* you?"

"I stopped going out with him—after one time."

"He angry?"

"I don't know. You never *knew* Ev. Strange guy."

"He ever threaten anyone?"

Suddenly Deborah stiffened. Her eyes quickly searched the room, as if looking for some support that wasn't there.

"Look, I don't want to talk," she said. "I mean, this could be trouble."

It wasn't really trouble for Deborah Stone, but Karlov understood. He sensed, at any rate, that she really had little to offer him. She'd fleshed out the material Jim Hurley had provided, and given him an additional insight into Everett Howe. Howe loomed even larger as a suspect, although all the "evidence" against him was conjecture. The key was linking him, or anyone, to the stolen gondolas.

"Ma'am, I won't ask you much more about the past," he said. "I can see how upset you are. But if you have any pictures from that night . . ."

"The night I went out with him?"

"No, ma'am, the night of the prom."

Now Deborah, increasingly apprehensive, wondering what she was being drawn into, threw Karlov one of the most skeptical looks he'd ever received, one that clearly said, I'm not sure if I trust you.

"It's confidential, Mrs. Stone," Karlov assured her.

"Well," Deborah replied, "I have prom pictures."

"I'd appreciate them," Karlov said. "We'll make copies and get them back to you fast. If you have any other school pictures, that could help."

"I might."

"Anything with . . . Howe."

"Oh no," Deborah protested. "That I don't have. No pictures of him. Look, he wasn't Mr. Popularity. I mean, if you saw him, you said hello. I told you, I went out with him once—to a bad movie." She got up and glided across the living room, disappearing into the back of the house to get the pictures Karlov wanted.

Deborah returned with a yearbook, a scrapbook, and a number of loose photos, most of them eight-by-ten glossies. On top of this batch was a Kodak-yellow box of thirty-five-millimeter slides. "I hate to let these out of my house," she told Karlov, placing them on a glass coffee table beside him. "This is my past."

"I'll guard them with my life," Karlov assured her. He leaned over the pictures, allowing his thin jacket lapels to flap forward. Deborah sat down next to him, also gazing at the confused pile of pictures in a way that she had never looked at them before. How could she have possibly known they might be *evidence,* might contain some clue to solve a crime, might provide the goods for a legal breakthrough? She really didn't want to admit it to herself—it was very unsophisticated to be thrilled—but, despite her fears, she was beginning to find this whole interview almost exciting, as if someone had thrust her into a movie. This was the most interesting thing to happen on her block since two people were tied up during a robbery.

Carefully, showing concern for the safety of the pictures, Karlov examined them one by one. The loose pictures were from the prom—pictures of groups of kids in rented tuxedos and purchased evening gowns, some with the clowning expressions of high school seniors about to be set free on the world, others trying to look so, so mature and unimpressed, too old before their time, the kind who usually messed up their marriages ten years later. In one photo Karlov could clearly see the young Deborah Stone, Deborah Green then, beaming at the camera, the well-liked teenager who sought approval from her classmates and received it, the girl never without a smile or a date.

And Karlov saw the gondolas—the little boats on tables, some with flowers sprouting out, others holding candies and popcorn, still others empty, providing part of the ambience. Karlov was mesmerized. Any one of those boats could have been at the head of any of the murder victims. It seemed incredible to him, almost unreal. Never had he looked directly at a clue in a murder case as it had appeared two decades earlier.

"May I now ask why those gondolas are important?" Deborah inquired.

"I'm afraid not," Karlov answered. "In fact, I'll ask you not to discuss my visit with *anyone*. It could damage us."

"I won't," Deborah replied.

"Uh, ma'am, could you provide names on all these people if I needed them?"

"I think I'd remember most. The others I could get."

Karlov began to gather up the pictures to take them back to Twentieth Precinct.

"Will I hear from you again?" Deborah asked.

"Aside from returning the pictures, I don't know, ma'am. Depends on what I need."

"Will I ever know what this is about?"

Karlov sighed. "You'll know, Mrs. Stone. God, will you know."

18

"**A**nd then there was this," Laura said, reaching into her Burberry's handbag and taking out a delicate gold chain. She handed it across the rickety metal table to Detective Rudolph Beer, who studied it closely.

"You've had this assessed?" Beer asked.

"Yes," Glen replied. "We wanted to see if it was actually gold. Hell, it is. Worth over two hundred dollars."

"A sizable sum," Beer agreed. "Especially for a bauble given, as it were, in the anonymous."

Rudolph Beer took a jeweler's eyepiece from his pocket and studied the chain, more for show than anything else. Beer was a detective of average ability, not known for either brilliance or acumen, but definitely known for a keen sense of public relations. If the department needed a man to convince the city that it was really "on" a case, they called Beer. At fifty years old, Beer busted his personal budget to buy the best clothes and shoes, and looked almost splendid—never a stain, never a crease, never a shirt that wasn't the finest fabric. Horn-rimmed glasses, a short Van Dyke beard and a bit of hair spray finished the "look," the image of success, one more suited to a psychiatrist than a New York detective. But crime victims loved it. It made them feel they were dealing with a man of authority. Beer never let them down. His pompous speech, his lawyerlike prose, would have sounded ludicrous coming from a less able practitioner. But Rudolph Beer had perfected the fine art of windbaggery, and played it to the hilt. He'd been assigned to Laura after Glen asked an old police contact to have a detective investigate the mysterious gifts. No one in the department took the case very seriously.

Glen, Laura and Beer sat in a conference room at main police headquarters near City Hall. It was a spare room, painted gray, with only the metal table at the center. The place gave Laura the creeps—like something out of a chain-gang movie—and she couldn't wait to get out. But Beer did impress her, as he meant to.

"This Jason Hebert," Beer asked, referring to little notes he kept on green three-by-five cards, "did he ever give you gifts, Ms. Barnett?"

"Oh, a few. A handbag once. But he wasn't a great gift giver."

"Do you know if he's come into some money?"

"I don't know."

"Ah. Has he made an effort to contact you since the relationship . . . ruptured?"

"No, I haven't heard from him."

"Ah. Do you have mutual friends?"

"No, we don't. For some reason, we never introduced each other to our friends. Jason was very private, very possessive."

"Wanted you to himself," Beer said.

"Yes."

"A familiar pattern. Most familiar. Now you must tell me, did this man every strike you?"

"No," Laura replied. "He was emotional, but nothing like that."

"Does either of you have any evidence whatever that this man Jason is indeed the person sending these gifts, to the exclusion of all other persons in the world?"

Glen barely held in a smile. Beer had obviously learned his barrister's approach by attending endless sessions in courtrooms. "That's the problem," Glen replied. "We really have no evidence, Detective Beer. As an attorney . . ."

Beer raised his hand. "Ah, not the time for legalities, counselor. This is the time for *inquiry*."

"Very well." Why argue with Sherlock Holmes?

"Now, when you first registered this complaint," Beer went on, "I asked one of my men to surveil this Jason Hebert. Odd fellow, isn't he?"

"Odd?" Laura asked.

"Not quite the well-dressed gentleman."

Laura smiled in a not-quite-fond remembrance of her time with Jason, how embarrassed she'd sometimes been when he refused even minimal neatness. "Jason never got over the sixties," she recalled. "He'll be the only hippie on Medicare."

"Humorous," Beer said.

Laura leaned forward, an urgent expression crossing her face. "What did your surveillance show?" she asked.

Beer paused. He loved the drama of moments like this. "An erratic lifestyle," he finally replied. "The professor has a number of lady friends, each one more, as they say, stoned, than the other."

"That's Jason."

"But that's also the problem," Beer went on. Now he got up and started pacing the room, each gesture of his arm designed for maximum effect. "You see, he seemed perfectly happy—not the type who would try to get back an old girlfriend by posting her anonymous gifts. Example: He made no trips to your neighborhood. The pining lover prefers to pine outside his old flame's residence. At minimum he would pass by. I'm sure you follow my logic."

"Yes."

"We'll keep an eye on him, and I want you to ring me if any more gifts arrive. But right now, I see no evidence that Jason Hebert is involved. I would ask you to search your memory, madam. Think if any men in the last year have looked your way with more than usual interest. Our suspect could easily be a delivery boy. And the entire episode may well turn out to be harmless. Men do these things. Sometimes it's a shy man, or a shy boy. Have you ever taught school?"

"No."

"My wife taught school. Occasionally, she'd get anonymous gifts from students. My wife is attractive, if I do say so."

"I'm sure," Laura said.

"I'd urge you simply to be careful and not become paranoid." Beer paused and smiled. He loved that word and used it whenever he could. "With us watching your Mr. Hebert, I doubt if you're in any special danger."

Beer, still pacing, looked down at Laura as a priest would look down at a frightened parishioner. He *was* reassuring, no doubt about that. He was also kissing off the whole thing, no doubt about that either, as Glen readily knew. Glen had done the same kissing off, although with considerably less style, when he was in the U.S. attorney's office. In fact, kissing off had become high art in law enforcement.

Beer promised to keep Laura informed if there were any change in Jason's behavior, or if he did make a secret visit to her block. At least Laura felt that someone was doing *something*. Beer knew how important that was to a crime victim, even one who might well be imagining the crime.

Glen and Laura left police headquarters and took a short walk past City Hall. Then they decided, at Glen's instigation, to take the Circle Line ferry around Manhattan. Maybe the diversion of a boat ride on a clear July day would help her.

For Laura, the time on the water with Glen, away from the traffic and pushing, was reminiscent of the days just after they'd first met—no problems, serenity, the calmness for which she yearned.

Laura hated the idea that she was burdening Glen with her fears about Jason. It seemed grossly unfair, a terrible intrusion into the relationship. And yet, Glen's very presence during this trauma made her realize, more than ever, how much she dreaded loneliness. What if Glen *weren't* there to help, to understand? What if she had only the walls to talk to? She remembered the days between Jason and Glen, when there was no one here, no one on the phone, no one to offer a thought or a comforting word. She pictured herself as strong, independent and more self-sufficient than her own mother had been. But she couldn't deny the sense of security, of protection, Glen brought her. Although she still continued to believe they should live apart, she always felt his presence.

Laura and Glen did think about the murders that had terrified their neighborhood, but the killings never became an obsession. Maybe they'd stopped, as the Zodiac killings had stopped in San Francisco. Or maybe the police were closing in on the killer.

That was someone else's problem.

19

It was time.

The repairman knew it. This was the time to call Laura, to talk with her again, to make the arrangements, to bring the dream one step closer to reality—just as he had with all the others. Laura was more special than the first ones, though. She was no compromise, no second choice to be picked simply because there was no other. He was excited about her, sure she'd be equally excited about him. He sat at his desk in the dark apartment, having just returned from work. The sun was still out, the sounds of kids playing in the street still vivid. What would those kids say, what would their parents say, if they knew what was going on inside that apartment?

He reached for his black Touch-tone phone and started tapping Laura's number, which he'd punched up on his Radio Shack TRS-80 computer. He hit each number precisely, emphasizing with every thrust of his index finger the meticulous care for which he had become known.

Laura's phone rang.

And again.

And then again.

She had to be home, the repairman thought. It was 6:20 P.M., and these women were always home just after work. It was always the best time to call.

Another ring.

Then a click.

"Hello, this is Laura Barnett. I can't come to the phone right now, but if you'll leave your name, number and the time you called, I'll phone you back. Wait for the beep. Thanks."

The repairman hung up. God knows, he didn't want his voice on a tape that might never be erased. So Laura would wonder who called and didn't leave a message. So what? It happened all the time. He'd simply call again later. But he wondered whether Laura was out with someone else, some man who fascinated her. No, that couldn't be. Life couldn't be *that* unfair.

He waited at his desk, skipping dinner, simply watching the small black Braun clock as the second hand swept around, time and time again. The image of Laura Barnett floated through his mind, flirting with him, teasing him, convincing him that she was part of his destiny. He didn't want to repeat his call too quickly. He didn't want to leave too many "blanks" on her answering machine, for then, when he did reach her, she might guess that he was the one who'd been afraid to leave messages. He had to appear strong, never shy, never afraid of anything.

* * *

He did try again at 8:15. This time the phone rang

once, then again, then a third time. He was about to hang up when he heard the receiver lifted.

"Hello?"

It was her.

"Uh, hello," he said, speaking slowly, yet forcefully. "I'm calling about your ad."

Laura became friendlier. "Oh yes, for the apartment."

"That's right. Is it still available?"

"Uh, yes."

The repairman's heart began to race. He craved these moments, craved them for themselves and for what they could lead to. "I wonder if you could give me some information—"

"I'd be glad to. My name is Laura Barnett. And you are?"

"Masters. Fred Masters," he lied. He hated to do it to Laura, but it was necessary. He'd make it up to her.

"Do you live here in town?" Laura asked.

"Uh, actually not. I'll be moving here pretty soon, but I visit a great deal." All right, so he lied again. But she'd understand when he had time to explain. She'd respect him.

"Transferred?"

"No, I'm starting a business here."

"I see." Laura was sitting in the kitchen. She had just returned with Glen, who was changing a light bulb. "What would you like to know?" she asked.

"About the building itself. I've heard such horror stories about New York co-ops."

Laura laughed. "Oh, you mean only wanting certain kinds of people."

"Yeah."

"Well, this isn't that kind of building. We have all types here. Most were here when it went co-op, so you don't get that attitude—only certain types need apply. We have store-owners, writers, some lawyers, even some retired people.''

The repairman barely heard. He was too busy imagining what Laura looked like at that very moment—maybe dressed in a light summer dress, her hair freshly washed, her nails polished, a picture of perfection.

''I like what I hear,'' the repairman said mechanically. ''Now, about the maintenance fees.'' He didn't care, but he just loved speaking with Laura.

''Right now they're four thirty-five a month, and that's low. They go up a little each year.''

''Do they have security guards in the building?''

''Oh no, that's not necessary,'' Laura replied. ''We're very safe here. You married?''

He hated the question. ''No,'' he said. ''Uh, I'd really like to see the place.''

''Fine. Will you be in New York for long?''

''A couple of weeks. What about a week from Saturday?''

Laura checked a huge calendar mounted on a bulletin board near the phone. ''Saturday looks fine. Are you sure it's good for you, Mr. Masters?''

''Yes, it's fine. About three in the afternoon?''

''Okay. Do you need any more information?''

''Well, the ad was pretty complete. I guess you have appliances.''

''Do I have appliances? Brand new refrigerator and dishwasher. Energy efficient. The stove isn't new, but it's gas and it works. By the way, there are washing machines on every floor.''

''Terrific.''

''All right, Mr. Masters, I'll see you a week from Saturday. Oh, you'd better give me your number in case I've got to change it.''

''Change it?''

"Well sometimes I have obligations."

A well of jealousy erupted inside the repairman. What kind of obligations? Was this a code word for a male friend? "Uh, I'm staying with people," he replied. "I don't like to bother them. Maybe I can call you Saturday morning to confirm."

"Well, okay. But if we're not home . . ."

If *we're* not home? Something was wrong here, something the repairman didn't like. "Maybe you have an answering machine," he said.

"Yes, I could leave a message on my machine. Right, I'll do that if anything happens. But I expect to be here."

"Thanks. I look forward to it."

The conversation ended. The repairman yearned for Laura Barnett, but feared the other half of the "we." Who was he? Or was it, could it be, a *she?* Maybe he had the whole thing completely mixed up. He'd find out. He *had* to find out. This one couldn't get away.

He could barely wait. But he knew Laura might present obstacles, difficulties that would take time to overcome. He had others on his list. He'd hoped to avoid them, to go straight to Laura. But he needed them. They had to be nurtured and used.

He snapped on his computer, the green screen lighting up the room in a sickly glow. Rubbing his right ear, he started going through the names, each name with a description, a history, a file. Some were approved for further action. Some were not. He always marveled at his own efficiency, his sense of organization.

*   *   *

Laura rushed into the living room and literally threw herself into Glen's arms, almost knocking him off balance. "Live one," she said. "I just feel it. No fast talk. No quick

money figures. He's moving here, so I *know* he's got to
have a place.''

Glen was beaming. The sooner the apartment was out
of the way, the sooner he and Laura could make firm plans.
''You·mentioned a week from Saturday at three.''

''He wanted that.''

''It kills our day, but—it's important. We'll work
around him. I'll be here.''

Laura looked at him oddly. ''Don't trust me, lawyer?''

''Sure I trust you. But, you know, I don't like the idea
of strange people coming up here alone.''

''I've had people look around.''

''I want to be here.''

Laura shrugged. ''Okay. Be here.''

She couldn't wait.

20

The *New York Post* called her one of the great new faces. It may have been an exaggeration, but not by much. Even the *Times* noted, in a more sober story, that she was considered a highly promising new model—someone to succeed Cheryl Tiegs or Christie Brinkley. But now she was gone, the latest victim of the serial killer who was menacing the West Side. Only twenty-three at her death, killed neatly, elegantly, with a single thrust of a sharp instrument to the heart.

She'd been known as scrupulously careful, almost paranoid. Someone with her looks would have to be cautious in a large, violent city. She would never have opened her door to a stranger or buzzed a stranger to come in from the outside. Yet it appeared that she'd opened her door willingly to the man who killed her.

Like the other victims, she'd been found with a little gondola at her head, pointed toward Winnetka, Illinois.

Leonard Karlov stared down at that gondola as if it had become some kind of curse, a symbol of his inadequacy. He was surrounded by uniformed officers of the Twentieth Precinct, but soon stepped away from them to take notes. The setting was so familiar—a one-bedroom apartment in an older building, no doorman, few amenities. In this apartment, though, there were pictures of the dead girl everywhere. Pictures taken by great photographers, pictures that had appeared in fashion magazines or department-store ads. Karlov thought he remembered some of those pictures. They haunted him, seemed to stare down at him as he made notes.

A patrolman presented an eighty-six-year-old woman to Karlov. She was the dead girl's next-door neighbor, and claimed to know something. Karlov had interviewed thousands of witnesses who "knew," so he could be excused his lack of enthusiasm for one who could barely see or stand.

"You have information for me, ma'am?" he asked.

"Oh yes," the lady replied in a strong voice that contradicted her years. "You want my name?"

"Yes, I do."

"*Miss* Vorspan. Please write it down."

"I will. Now, Miss Vorspan, I understand you live next door."

"For forty years."

"You knew the deceased, Sabrina Brent?"

"Of course I knew her! We called her Sasha. Such a terrible, terrible thing. But these young girls, they have funny friends. In my time, my mother would pick my friends. Not these girls. So this happens."

"Yes, ma'am. Did you see or hear anything last night?"

"I heard her doorbell. About eight o'clock."

"And after that?"

"I heard the door open and close."

"Did you hear conversation?"

The ancient lady glared at Karlov, as if the detective had deeply offended her. "I don't listen in," she snapped. "I got class."

"Of course. What I mean is, did you hear voices only?"

"Oh. I see what it is y'mean. Yeah, voices. Sasha. She had a very pretty voice, I'm sure. Then there was a man."

"Anything special about the man's voice?"

"I couldn't tell."

"Was there arguing?"

"I heard her drop."

"But was there arguing?"

"Toward the end, I heard her say somethin' about complaining."

Karlov perked up. "Complaining?"

"I didn't eavesdrop."

"I *know* that. What did she say?"

"It was somethin' like, 'I'll complain.' "

"To who?"

Again the old lady glared. "You must think I had m'ear on the wall."

"Miss Vorspan, I don't think anything. I'm trying to solve a murder. Now, if you can only remember who she said she'd complain to."

"Superior."

"What does that mean?"

"She'd complain to."

"She'd complain to the man's superiors," Karlov said. Miss Vorspan shrugged. She really wasn't sure.

But to Karlov it seemed to fit. It was a common

ıdiom—to complain to another's superiors, to go to the boss, to get someone in trouble for some infraction.

But who?

Who were the superiors?

The lady didn't know, and Karlov had no guesses. Miss Vospan could provide only the additional piece of information—that she'd heard a loud squeak coming from Sabrina Brent's apartment. She'd never heard it before, and couldn't identify it.

As usual, the killer had taken the deceased's calendar. Sabrina had undoubtedly written down her appointment with the killer, but now the record was gone.

But she'd written it somewhere else. And the killer hadn't discovered it.

Sabrina had a small notepad/calendar that she'd kept, of all places, in her shower. It was plastic, and she wrote on it with a special waterproof pen. She'd made a note for eight o'clock on the night she was murdered. It read CALL BACK.

Now Karlov had a word, and absolutely no idea what it meant. It rolled over and over in his mind, tearing at him, bullying him, defying definition, explanation, even logical guessing. He *assumed* that Sabrina had to phone back the man who visited her, but why did she make a note to do it at the time he was visiting? And if she had to phone him back at all, why hadn't she written his phone number?

Karlov took the latest gondola back to the Twentieth Precinct and melted it down. There was nothing new— Chicago newspaper from June of 1964, and a strip of one newspaper from Winnetka. As far as he could see, the murder of Sabrina Brent had produced not one new piece of usuable evidence.

Karlov pondered the squeak from the Brent apartment, and theorized that it was furniture being moved. Maybe

Sabrina had asked her visitor to help her move something. A check of the apartment did show scuff marks in several places, and Karlov knew it was hardly unusual for young women to rearrange things.

* * *

"I see congratulations are in order."

"Yes . . . I guess they are."

"Then may I . . ."

Rudolph Beer, detective, New York Police Department, hardened veteran of hundreds of homicides, rapes and bludgeonings, lifted Laura Barnett's hand and actually kissed it.

Laura Barnett was wearing an engagement ring.

She and Glen had decided that the time was right, that they were both sure, that they simply could not allow the mystery of anonymous gifts to interfere. It would eat them up, they realized, if life suddenly stopped until the "donor" was identified.

Rudolph Beer sat down on Laura's couch, facing both Laura and Glen, and took a small, leather-bound pad from his suit pocket. He'd come to report on his investigation of the gifts and what, if anything, it had turned up. He was genuinely delighted that Laura and Glen had announced their engagement. He felt, in a strange way, that *he* had something to do with it, that he had reassured them, given them a degree of strength.

"I know you'll both be very happy," he said, leafing through his little notebook. "You complement each other very well."

"Thank you," Laura said, gazing over at Glen.

Glen just nodded. He knew Beer was all words.

"Now," Beer said, "there has been one anonymous gift since the gold chain."

"Yes," Laura replied. "The one I called you about—the scarf."

"*Red* scarf."

"Yes. I've seen scarves like it at Saks, but there was no store name on the box."

"I'm sure," Beer said. "But we did survey the major stores, madam. Many red scarves of the brand you gave us have been sold, mostly for cash. It would be virtually impossible to trace each buyer, but we *are* trying."

"We appreciate that," Glen said.

"But I must caution you, the scarf could have been bought out of town. Even in another country. It is, in fact, an import. Results cannot be guaranteed."

"We understand," Glen agreed. He'd never seen acting like this.

"Now, as far as your Mr. Jason Hebert," Beer went on, "I must say again that he does prefer the company of rather . . . imaginative women."

Laura could only agree. She remembered Jason saying that she was the only normal woman he'd ever pursued, which may have been why he found her so fascinating.

"And you may be interested to know that the gentleman did in fact visit this neighborhood."

Suddenly Laura tensed. She feared what was coming next, what bombshell Beer was about to drop.

"However, it was only to get a television repaired," Beer said. "There's an authorized service station up here. I've used it myself."

"I see," Laura replied, a note of apprehension in her voice. "Could he also have . . . passed by here?"

"No, in fact he didn't. And he hasn't mailed any packages, as best we can see."

"Maybe that was something your people missed," Glen said, a bit bluntly.

Beer was offended. Like the conductor of a great orchestra, he didn't like to be challenged. "Sir," he said, enunciating each word carefully, "there is very little we miss."

Glen said nothing. Beer knew his turf and how to defend it.

"We are going to remove our surveillance of Jason Herbert," Beer announced.

Laura was visibly upset. "Isn't it too early?" she asked, looking to Glen for support.

"We simply can't continue it," Beer replied. "There's been no crime. There's no indication of a crime. We see no prospect of a crime. From a departmental standpoint, it can't be justified."

"I see," Laura said.

Glen nodded his understanding. Of course Beer was right. How could he be anything *but* right? Glen had warned Laura earlier that there wasn't much substance to her complaint, and now he felt slightly humiliated. He knew, but would not hurt Laura by saying, that only *his* influence got the surveillance in the first place.

"I'm sure you'll be safe," Beer said.

* * *

A day later, Laura and Glen went up to Zabar's, the renowned delicatessen, where foods, exotic smells, utensils and cooking gadgets are packed in with people who have to get their "Zabar's fix" to make the week complete. Glen was determined to have his salami, which Laura was convinced would ultimately kill him, but which *he* felt was a major source of his well-being and happiness.

The din was semi-deafening, the sight of the delicacies irresistible. Laura and Glen took a number and waited in line, taking in the banter between customers and countermen.

The counter workers were self-appointed experts on the whole world in general and supreme authorities on how much corned beef was needed to serve six in particular, if each person had two sandwiches except the one on a diet who'd have a half.

They were there almost ten minutes when Laura turned to examine a copper pot on sale. In the corner of her eye she caught a glimpse of a man. Even without seeing more than part of his face, she knew.

She nudged Glen, nervously, warily. "Jason," she whispered.

In the next instant, Jason saw her. But he quickly looked away, disgusted.

He rushed out of the store.

Laura was shaking.

She felt the knot inside her all day.

21

Glen tried to comfort Laura during the rest of the day and into the evening, to get her mind off Jason. There were wedding plans to discuss, and a honeymoon trip they both wanted.

But there was something else, something unexpected.

It came in the midst of some music on the radio that Glen had turned on to provide a soothing background. Soft music. Love songs.

"We interrupt this program to bring you a news bulletin—"

Laura and Glen stopped talking and both turned to the radio as if it were a TV. There were a few seconds of silence, and then the deep voice of a seasoned announcer. What followed brought instant relief to Laura and Glen, just as it brought relief to an entire city.

They had him.

"Police tonight announced the arrest of Everett Howe in connection with the murders of—"

They had him. The serial murderer was caught, in custody. The young women of the West Side were safe. Leonard Karlov had picked the right man.

The news spread like a shot through a city certain that another woman would inevitably die in her own apartment. Every radio and television station but one broke programs to make the announcement, the one exception being a station that was running the highest rated evening soap opera. The *New York Post* snapped its presses into action and rushed a special edition with a red stripe across the top of the front page: HE'S CAUGHT! Each politician from the mayor on down issued public statements of thanksgiving, praise for the police and summaries of what he'd done to advance the investigation. The controller came up with an immediate dollar cost for the capture.

The archbishop called for forgiveness for the soul of the accused.

Reporters crowded into a small room in the office of the Brooklyn district attorney, Manuel S. Barber, late of the State Assembly, a man who understood what solving a major case could mean in a race for governor. He'd patterned himself after former governor Thomas E. Dewey, who'd used the prosecutor's office to catapult himself to positions of serious power, but Barber never mentioned Dewey—it was forbidden in his office. He didn't want to be compared with a man who'd ultimately lost.

Barber was smallish, in his late forties, and rocked backward and forward while speaking, almost like an old man at prayer. Now was the moment of his glory, standing in the TV lights, in the required shirtsleeves, flanked by a police captain and a sergeant, reinforced by a deputy commissioner behind him and the controller of the city of New York, who showed up because he always showed up.

"Ladies and gentlemen," be began, "I have good news. Our police have captured the man who has paralyzed the city for so many weeks. His name is Everett Morton Howe, a murderer with a long history of mental problems. He was captured here in Brooklyn while attempting to break into a woman's apartment.

"Howe is now in custody and will be arraigned tomorrow morning before Judge Alan S. Bernstein. The circumstances of the arrest . . ."

*　　*　　*

Leonard Karlov was working late that night, which means he was working regular hours. On his desk: mountains of documents culled from the personal files of the murder victims. Maybe there was something he'd missed. Maybe there was some hint of the killer's lifestyle, of some contact he'd had with his victims. Karlov had made the Winnetka connection, the Howe connection, yet he still didn't have a man in custody.

He started reviewing each document, each little note, each jotting in each margin, his eyes bloodshot and stinging from the constant search. The phone on his desk rang. Bad news. Phone calls in the night only brought bad news.

"Karlov."

"Relax," said the voice. "It's over."

A sergeant from downstairs gave Karlov the news—that Everett Howe had been captured by a team of detectives in Brooklyn. Brooklyn hadn't even extended Karlov the courtesy of a call, an invitation to come over and share in the honor. Brooklyn took it all. No one remembers the cops who don't catch the guy, and Leonard Karlov wasn't important to Manuel Barber's political career.

Karlov remained stunned by the news as the sergeant rattled off some details.

"What've they got?" Karlov demanded.

"Uh, the perpetrator tried to break into the apartment of an old girlfriend. Used all kinds of special keys and gadgets. A real tool man, this one. A neighbor heard and called our guys."

"Go on." Instinctively, Karlov didn't want it to be over. It was natural, normal, a cop's obsession with solving the case he started.

"Uh, the guy seemed to know a lot about the homicides in Manhattan."

"Doesn't tell me anything."

The sergeant continued. "Uh, I think I heard that one witness *thinks* he saw him inside the building of the last deceased."

"What kind of witness?"

"Uh, sir, I just got the call. I don't know what . . ."

"Okay," Karlov said. "Thanks."

He hung up and leaned back in his chair, which squeaked as if sharing his private agony. He knew the sergeant had only the partial story, that Brooklyn undoubtedly had the case against Howe nailed down, but something didn't ring true: when a major criminal is captured, the police always boast about the *single* clue that clinched the case. Why didn't the sergeant know about that? Was there one, or did Brooklyn truly stumble onto Howe when he was trying to break into that apartment? And why no mention of the gondolas? They couldn't be a secret any longer, not with Howe caught. The gondolas were too unique for the Brooklyn DA not to mention. They were real color, real crime melodrama.

But it was no use.

They had him. It *was* all over.

Karlov turned on the radio, hearing the news the city had first heard many minutes earlier.

"and the mayor now here, congratulating each of the detectives involved in the capture . . ."

He turned off the radio.

He'd developed all the leads. He'd traced the crimes back to Winnetka. He'd worked with Jim Hurley in Chicago. *He'd* made the connection with Everett Howe. And now His Honor the Mayor was congratulating Brooklyn, and Leonard Karlov again felt like an outsider, like the little Russian, which someone once called him in the police academy.

He stared at the pile of papers, the legacy of murdered women. Brooklyn hadn't even gone through them. And, without giving it much thought, he rushed out of his office, down the precinct stairs and into his own car.

He raced to Brooklyn.

*   *   *

The press conference was still going on when Karlov arrived. Outside the room, the Brooklyn cops were milling around. They knew him. Karlov saw some of the little smiles, the "we won" smirking. He saw Alvin Washington, sergeant of detectives, massive, black, an old friend from Manhattan who'd been transferred to this police Siberia after complaining about a racial slur. Washington was fair, Karlov knew. He wouldn't gloat, he wouldn't feel any particular loyalty to Brooklyn. Karlov approached him.

"Al . . ."

"Hey, Len, how goes?"

"My case just got cleared."

"Oh yeah, that was yours. I remember."

"Hey, Al, what have they really got?"

"Paper and ink, baby."

"Confession?"

"Yeah."

"How many times they hit him?"

Washington looked at Karlov, saw the fatigue in his eyes, and didn't answer. He couldn't answer, and Karlov knew it.

"Any hard stuff?" Karlov went on.

"Circumstances. The paper and ink is the best they've got."

That didn't satisfy Karlov. He'd seen a lot of paper and ink in his career, a lot of it thrown out by courts suspicious of quick "confessions."

It took Karlov six hours to tunnel through the bureaucracy. He wanted one shot at Howe, one chance to question him, one session to satisfy *himself*.

Brooklyn was hesitant. This was their collar, their prize, their ticket to greater power. Why let Karlov in on the victory? What had he done for Brooklyn?

And yet, there was another side to police politics. What if they denied him, after all the coverage he'd received in the press? What would it look like?

And so Leonard Karlov, at 5:15 in the morning, his eyes blurred from lack of sleep, found himself in a heavily guarded jail cell in Brooklyn, facing the accused, Everett Morton Howe, who had a constant, stupid grin behind a beard he was trying to grow to disguise his face.

So this was Howe.

This was the enigma from Skokie, the boy, now the man, first fingered by Jim Hurley, then let go by Sean Finney. Of course, Karlov had come face to face with wanted suspects many times in his career, but he felt a special fascination with this one, this man with the deranged mind who apparently killed with such ease, such finesse.

And he was grinning, as if he were proud of it all.

Karlov had read Howe's confession. It had mentioned the gondolas.

Karlov didn't even bother to say hello. He had no small talk for Howe, no little words to formally introduce him to the jurisdiction of the New York Police Department. He could see that Howe had already tinkered with the bed in his cell—fixing a leg that was loose and ready to come off. Karlov made a mental note to caution the guards: this man had the potential to escape. His twisted mental state did not interfere with his mechanical ability.

"Why'd you put the gondolas at their heads?" Karlov asked Howe.

"'Cause it was cute," Howe answered, in a voice much deeper than Karlov had expected.

"Cute?"

"I thought it was cute."

"Why'd you point 'em toward Illinois?"

"'Cause I come from there."

"Where'd you get the gondolas?"

Howe shrugged, as if the answer was too obvious for bother. "Where *would* I get 'em? I bought 'em in a toy store."

For a moment, Leonard Karlov just stared at the accused.

* * *

An hour later, charges were dropped against Everett Howe. Toy stores don't sell papier-mâché gondolas made in Winnetka, Illinois, in 1964.

Karlov never did find out who'd prompted Howe about the gondolas, who'd fed him the information. No one, even his friends in the department, would say.

Politics.

High politics.

And he never did find out what new sickness prompted Howe to confess to crimes he hadn't committed. Although charges against Howe stemming from the serial kilings had been dropped, Howe was still held in connection with his escape from a California mental facility.

In a way, Karlov was crushed by Howe's innocence, just as he'd been incensed that Howe had been captured by Brooklyn. Howe had been the centerpiece of his theory about the case. Now he was gone, and Leonard Karlov was left without a single suspect. What was worse, he was left without any credible, new theory about the serial murders. They were still killings without any apparent motive, without any apparent link. He felt a more intense pressure than ever before, for he knew that the Howe episode had created a major flap within the department and had humiliated city officials. Of course, he shed no tears over the egg on Brooklyn's collective face, and he saw Manuel Barber as dead meat in the city's politics. But he knew the public outcry over the mistaken arrest would be immediate, and that the papers would scream for police scalps.

He was back on the case.

But it was *his* scalp on the line.

Karlov got no sleep.

He raced back to his office in the Twentieth Precinct. No lovely sight, he rushed into the precinct house, unshaven, his suit crumpled, his shirt showing a severe case of ring-around-the collar, his tie pulled down, his shoulders rounded. This was not the image of a public protector, the picture of a popular cop. He could not avoid the turned backs as he walked to his office. He'd challenged an arrest by the department; he'd subjected the department to negative publicity, even to ridicule, certainly to scathing editorials in the press. He wasn't one of them, and he felt it more than ever before.

Yet no one would think of taking him off the case. No one in the department, no matter how much they resented what he'd done in Brooklyn——embarrassing the department—— would want responsibility for that.

When he entered his office, he was startled to find Harold Kramer, in a business suit and silk tie.

"What the hell are you doing here?" Karlov asked, sinking into his chair with the dull thud of a falling body.

"Making sure you're alive," Kramer answered, a broad smile now revealing most of his chins.

"Well, what's the verdict?"

"You're alive—barely. I'm surprised."

"Hal," Karlov said, the irony dancing around each word, "you didn't think the dedicated officers of this department would *do* something to me, did you?"

"Yes."

"Like what?"

"Like bottling parts of you for sale at my supermarket, that's what. Jesus Christ, Len, have you been watching the tube, or listening to radio?"

"I got some hints."

"I mean, last night they were giving out Nobel Prizes for detective work and then comes Karlov. You are not popular in the Brooklyn precincts, Len. I've got friends in the Brooklyn coroner's office. They tell me the cops are bringing in bodies this morning with *your* name written on 'em."

Karlov leaned back and closed his eyes, trying to feel immune, not quite making it. "I did what I had to do."

"I know," Kramer said softly. "That's why I'm here. There are friends left."

Karlov was touched by Kramer's concern. The Medical Examiner's office was intensely political, and Kramer could be hurting himself by associating with the man who sank Brooklyn's moment of glory. Here was a real friend. He'd seen precious little of friendship in his career.

The two talked for a few minutes about the tumult of

the night before, Karlov took a few calls from inquiring reporters, and then reality sank back in.

"Hal," Karlov said, "I'm facing the old law: time destroys investigations. The guy leaves nothing of importance when he kills. The key is something that happened out in Illinois in 1964. You know how cold that trail is?"

"I can guess. So what's next?"

Karlov gestured toward the papers on his desk. "I'm going through the girls' papers," he said. "Somewhere there's got to be *something*. Hal, they *knew* this man. They let him in."

"Ever think it might be some delivery guy? They'd let in a delivery guy."

"I've covered it. To have something delivered, you've got to call. Maybe pizza. Maybe those new ice cream places. We've checked every establishment on the West Side that delivers. There are no records of deliveries to these girls, and no evidence that records were destroyed. Also, there's evidence that the visits were long—long enough to have a Coke. A delivery guy? I doubt it."

"Mind if I hang around while you dig?" Kramer asked.

"No. But looking at a guy with no sleep go through a pile of canceled checks and Bloomingdale's receipts might not be too exciting."

"Better than corpses," Kramer said.

"Yeah."

"Hey Len, you just said something interesting. Department store receipts. You know, when you use a credit card, they usually make you put down your address. Could this be some guy from a store . . ."

"Checked it out," Karlov replied. "First, it's unlikely a guy from a store would be invited in, same as with a delivery boy. Second, we checked every computer in the universe. These victims did shop in a few of the same stores, but none of them had purchases around the time of the murders. Also, how would a guy from a store get upstairs? He'd have to be buzzed up, and these women were careful. Everyone said that. It doesn't fit the pattern. I won't rule it out, though.''

"So, *you* have any ideas?" Kramer asked.

"A few," Karlov replied, yawning a yawn that revealed a lifetime of dental work. "A park friend."

"A what?"

"Park friend. All these women lived on the West Side, not far from a park. Central Park. Riverside Park. There are guys who spend time in those parks. They feed the pigeons. They give candy to kids. Sometimes they get into conversations. Someone like that might not show up in the victims' history. They might not have even mentioned a guy they met in the park."

"But would they let him up? Someone they just met . . . ?"

"You've got the wrong idea," Kramer said. "These aren't bums. Most of them are retired. They like the park—and it *is* nice weather."

"I ask again, professor, would they let him up?"

"Yeah. They would. What if he was a kind, pathetic guy. He appears at the intercom and asks to come up. Says he needs a favor. She's talked to him in the park, maybe feels sorry for him."

"This might fit," Kramer said. "But the manner of death . . ."

"Yeah, that gets me too," Karlov replied. "Those were strong thrusts."

"It may not be a great problem," Kramer theorized. "Even an old man can be strong and quick, especially if he's emotionally excited. We had a case a year ago where an eighty-six-year-old man beat his wife to death—I mean with fists, no weapons. It *is* possible.''

''I've got it on my list. I'm having our guys check every park for regulars.''

''Other theories?'' Kramer asked.

''Dial services.''

''Oh, Jesus.''

''Hal, you never know. Clean-cut girls, all-American, but you just never know what went on in their minds. They could have called...''

''Male escorts.''

''Call 'em anything you want. *That's* the kind of thing you just can't trace. Records have a strange way of disappearing.''

''Old guys in parks and gigolos. The world of New York glamour.''

Again, Karlov eyed the pile of papers. ''I'm going to work,'' he said. ''Those are only theories. Between you, me and the Brooklyn DA, I hope they're wrong. I don't want to ruin those girls' memories.''

Harold Kramer relaxed in the office as Karlov took each piece of paper from the files of brutally murdered women and studied it. The files—some of which were simply shoe boxes—told the stories of the girls' lives.

''Amazing what clothes cost,'' Karlov said. ''Maybe I'm behind the times, but there are receipts here—I mean, sixty bucks for a pair of jeans. I buy jeans, Levis, downtown, maybe twenty bucks.''

''You *are* behind the times,'' Kramer said. ''They bought designer jeans.''

''Mine aren't designed? Who decided on two legs and a zipper?''

Kramer laughed. ''Yeah. But...designer means *designer*, a guy who goes to discos and talks funny.''

Karlov returned to the files. "We checked out building staffs," he said, as if to no one in particular. "We thought maybe that some handyman was going from building to building, or maybe some painter. No luck."

Karlov began rambling about all the false leads, the theories, the suggestions from mystery writers, former policemen, private detectives, even members of the Sherlock Holmes society in New York. Any that seemed plausible were checked out. He'd even tracked down a rumor that all the girls secretly knew a famous network anchorman. It turned out to be just that—a rumor. And no fewer than 385 names had arrived anonymously by mail—men, the senders said, who were probably mass murderers. A few names had been repeated four and five times in different envelopes.

Some people, Karlov often mused, would do almost anything to settle a grudge.

Then, as he was going through the papers of Carol Krindler, the fourth girl murdered, Karlov suddenly stopped. He gazed at one slip, and tilted his head as if the new angle would give him a different perspective. He picked up the slip, a bit larger than a three-by-five card, and studied it. Kramer detected Karlov's sudden interest.

"A bite?" Kramer inquired.

Karlov shrugged. He was so weary that the paper before him seemed a blur, and he had to strain to read each word.

"So?" Kramer asked, nudging him.

"I've seen this," Karlov answered. "It was in one of the other files."

"What is it?"

"A receipt."

"Store?"

"No, newspaper."

"Subscription?"

"No, for an ad. Carol Krindler placed it. She was thinking of moving, and advertised her co-op. The bill is for sixty-two forty-five. I'm sure I saw a bill like this for one of the other girls."

Karlov flipped some papers and came up with another bill to Carol Krindler for an apartment ad. "Maybe this is what I saw," he mumbled. "No, no, I really think it was somewhere else."

He reached for another pile of papers, stacked neatly at the corner of his desk. He began going through them, and Kramer suddenly noticed that Karlov's pace was accelerating. The papers were moving faster, Karlov's tired eyes coming alive once more, clicking from side to side. Kramer knew what was in Karlov's gut. This was a connection, possibly, this had been overlooked, possibly, this was a new angle . . . possibly.

Then, Karlov stopped.

"Sure," he said, a slight, crooked smile coming to his dry lips, "there it is. Debby Moore. Remember? The second girl murdered."

"Sure."

"She also advertised. She owned a little apartment in Queens that her parents bought for her. She wanted to sell it. There's an ad receipt here."

"I'm not feeling this is earth-shaking news," Kramer said.

"It might not be," Karlov conceded, "but it might be." He became silent, and started going through other papers from the other girls. Now Kramer wanted to stay, wanted to see where this would lead.

Karlov's hands were quick, and his body was enjoying a second wind. He didn't have to study each document. The ad receipts had a characteristic blue margin that could be spotted easily. The only sound in the room was the crackling of papers, interspersed with an occasional grumble from Karlov as he gave himself a paper cut.

A pile of papers fell off the desk. Karlov stared at them, more hurt than angry, as if the little slips had betrayed him. Kramer picked them up.

"Another one," Karlov said. "Constance Rainey. They told me she was thinking of selling. She placed two ads."

"What do you think?" Kramer asked.

"I'm afraid to think yet."

"Why did they keep those receipts, anyway?"

"They had them in their tax files. I remember something about that. If you sell your home, the expenses in selling are tax-deductible, including advertising. Some guy who does taxes told me."

"So three girls had receipts. So what?"

"Three out of five—so far," Karlov said. "Young women. How many young women get involved in real estate transactions?"

"Not too many."

"I'm going through more papers."

Karlov continued. He hadn't yet examined the files of Marie Gould, the third victim, and Sabrina Brent, the fifth. He knew what he was looking for. If he found it, the case could blow open. "When people advertise," he said, "other people visit . . . and they're admitted."

"Yeah," Kramer said, and the tension in the room crackled. "How come you didn't notice this before?"

"Every time you look at a piece of evidence," Karlov explained, "you see something different. Your thinking evolves. It changes. It's like seeing a great movie over and over. You see new things every time."

He kept searching. He felt like a voyeur. He remembered his father's tales—how the KGB would go through people's records, how a little scrap of paper could mean an all-expense-paid trip to Siberia. It wasn't right to inspect the records of innocent, dead women. There was something immoral about it. Gentlemen didn't read other people's mail, he recalled an American diplomat having said. But at least this was for a good cause.

Sabrina Brent's papers were the most fascinating—as one would expect of a model running on New York's fast track. There were telephone numbers for the leading fashion designers, notes from celebrities, even a bill for cosmetic surgery on her right hand. And there were press clippings—Sabrina at a benefit, Sabrina with a leading actor, Sabrina playing a bit part in a soap opera. Karlov didn't much identify with this aspect of New York. He was a stay-at-home who rarely ventured out of his neighborhood, the Riverdale section of the Bronx, except for work. This was another world, and he had no particular desire to enter it.

"Here it is," he finally said, quietly, as if he had expected it all along. "She advertised."

"In New York?" Kramer asked.

"Jersey."

"Jersey?"

"She rented a little studio there. When she moved here she sublet it. She had to advertise for that."

"That makes me a little skeptical," Kramer said.

"Why?"

"It's Jersey. Let's say some guy came up and visited her, looking over the apartment . . ."

"Yeah?"

"She was killed in New York. She didn't advertise in New York. No one visited her here."

Karlov stared back at the ad receipt. Kramer was right, of course. Two of the girls had not advertised the apartments in which they were murdered—Deborah Moore, who'd moved from Queens, and Sabrina Brent. And both of these women had been killed months after their ads ran.

Of course, someone could have seen their apartments in the other areas and traced the women to Manhattan. After all, finding out someone's new address is relatively easy. But how could he have been admitted? The killer got in easily, and he got in at night.

And how did the killer know that the women would be alone?

There were too many questions, too many contradictions. Someone answering a real-estate ad could conceivably be admitted easily simply by saying he was interested in the apartment. But if he wanted to kill, he'd do it then.

And what about Marie Gould? Karlov found no receipts for her. A quick call to the largest newspaper, though, revealed that she had indeed advertised her apartment, but only once. None of her friends had mentioned her wish to move. Maybe it had been a spur of the moment thing. Maybe she'd just been testing the market. Maybe she hadn't wanted anyone to know. Sometimes people are secretive about their moving plans.

"What now?" Kramer asked.

"More searching," Karlov replied. He wanted to go through *all* the papers in the victims' files. He could find some note, some phone number, that could provide a further clue.

What Karlov found was mail. One of the things that death doesn't stop is mail. The deceased receive mail weeks, months, even years after death. And in each victim's mail Karlov found flyers from real-estate agents. They were the usual high-pressure jobs—now is the time to buy, now is the time to sell, last chance, won't last, do it now or else. Karlov had always lumped real-estate agents with piano salesmen, used-car dealers and kids who sold Omega watches for eighteen dollars on the corner of Forty-second and Seventh . . . except the kids were more pleasant.

The flyers clinched it. These young women all had active relationships with real-estate people. True, they'd advertised their apartments themselves, but it was common for brokers to read private ads, then call the party and offer their services. That's how real-estate brokers got listings. The ad receipts, and now the flyers, were solid links between the victims—the links for which Karlov had been searching.

Karlov realized that the murderer might not have been a buyer who came to the victims' apartments, but a real-estate agent, perhaps one who became involved in real estate specifically so he could visit young, single women.

He went home and slept fifteen hours. Some things simply could not be put off.

23

Laura and Glen weren't even sure what kind of wedding they wanted, but Laura started making preliminary plans anyway. She and Glen would pay for it themselves. Laura's father was an administrator with the Justice Department in Washington and her mother was a librarian. They'd already helped with Laura's apartment and were putting Laura's younger brother through college. It wasn't fair to ask them to do more. Besides, independent women shouldn't write home for money. That was the way Laura felt.

She'd always thought that the most important thing about a wedding, aside from the ceremony itself, was the memory, and memory meant pictures. She'd passed a photo studio in her neighborhood many times and had admired the work displayed in the window—candid, joyful, sometimes funny, the kind of pictures that could bring back memories year after year. She was determined that this photographer would do her wedding, no matter how small it was. And so, after work on Wednesday, she checked in at the apartment and started walking toward The Snap Shop, which remained open until nine each evening so the Lauras of the neighborhood could come in, study the samples and place their orders.

Laura loved strolling the West Side streets in the shadows of late afternoon. She loved the elderly people who sat outside apartment buildings trying to have some social contact with an ever-more-youthful world. She loved the singles who packed into the new restaurants, seeking social contacts of a different order. She loved the kids, the remnants of minority groups that were being squeezed out—snapping rubber balls against stoops in that ancient New York ritual of summer. She was amused by the yuppies—walking briskly from midtown jobs, wearing their Sony Walkmen and Nike running shoes, panic etched in their faces as they plotted the next day's escapades on the fast track. Most of all, she actually enjoyed the noise—the honking horns, the chatter along the sidewalks, the music coming from brownstones, the chronic sirens. She hated uninterrupted quiet.

As she walked, she thought about Jason and those gifts. Maybe they *were* someone's prank. Or maybe she did have some secret admirer who was just too shy to come forward. The police report on Jason had been so clean that she couldn't go on just assuming that he'd been the sender. In the excitement over the coming wedding, the gifts were becoming nothing more than a bizarre curiosity anyway. She hoped they'd just stop coming.

And she thought about the serial killer. As she walked, her eyes were everywhere. She walked toward the outside of the sidewalk, as city people generally do, having aways been told that muggers can grab a woman from the alleyways between buildings. The police had messed up in Brooklyn, and she realized that the killer might still be in the neighborhood. But she was careful, she told herself. She could never become a victim—after all, she took every conceivable precaution. And she wasn't seeing or even admitting any young men but Glen. She feared for some woman who might be the next victim. But she knew it wouldn't be her.

She passed within half a block of a man wearing sunglasses, carrying a Nikon camera and a two-hundred-millimeter telephoto lens. No one noticed the photo nuts. They were all over New York. As she passed close to him, he rubbed his right ear vigorously, then clicked off a picture. Laura wasn't even watching.

She walked into the Snap Shop and found herself the only customer amidst walls of photos, black-and-white and color, some with blue ribbons denoting prizes in picture competitions.

The man with the Nikon and long lens appeared across the street some moments later, and Laura saw him out of the corner of her eye. A ridiculous juxtaposition, she thought: the little amateur with his oversized rig and these magnificent photographs by a respected craftsman.

Mr. Windemere—that was the only name he used—stepped out from behind a partition that separated the back of the shop from the display section. He was a bulbous figure with a totally bald head and a little beard, and he insisted on wearing a uniform of green shorts and knee socks. "Of service?" he asked Laura, with a touch of a twinkle.

"Oh, I'm getting married," Laura replied, surprised by Mr. Windemere's appearance. "I'll need some pictures."

"Fantastical," Mr. Windemere replied, breaking out in

a giddy smile. He oozed enthusiasm from every happy little pore.

"I like your candids," Laura went on, not quite sure how to start a conversation with Mr. Windemere.

"I'm glad you enjoy them," Mr. Windemere replied. "You'll notice the awards. I love being loved."

"Yes, yes. Very impressive."

"If you want something out of the ordinary, not just the boring wedding snaps . . ."

"Yes, exactly."

"Let me show you the hot stuff."

So Mr. Windemere went to the back room to get out the standard sales piece, and every few moments the man with the Nikon photographed *her*, then turned away to be unobtrusive, then rubbed his right ear.

But Laura was too taken with Mr. Windemere and his photos to notice or care.

*   *   *

The repairman had never done it before.

He'd never photographed his victims before visiting them.

But this one was special, and he wasn't at all sure that she'd be a victim. She could be the *one* to survive, if only she'd be reasonable.

He developed the pictures himself in a makeshift darkroom that he had set up in his apartment. As each one emerged under the stark orange light, he studied the face with the care a fine sculptor gives his model. She *was* magnificent. Those eyes. Those bright, dominating eyes. None of the other women had those eyes. He'd be looking into them soon, looking into them from a few inches away. Too bad if they had to be shut forever. Too bad if they had to show fear and terror in some last, anguished moment.

There was one photo he particularly liked. Laura was looking almost directly at his lens, but he'd been so far away that she probably hadn't noticed. The picture showed her smiling, apparently reacting to some photo she'd seen on Mr. Windemere's wall. The repairman always wanted to see her smile. Or, if it came to that, he wanted at least to *remember* her smiling.

When the pictures dried, he carefully cut Laura's head from each one, and put these portraits in his wallet—the only pictures he carried. He felt close to her, and took the wallet out frequently to look at her face.

He was no different from any other guy who kept precious pictures with him all the time.

24

Your Castle was the name of one of those real
estate agencies that Karlov loved to hate. Here was a level
of exaggerated claims, distortion of fact, and general deception exceeded only by certain missions to the United Na-
tions and a few large law firms. Your Castle didn't sell
many castles—two-bedroom apartments without moat were
more in their line—but the doors to the agency on Queens
Boulevard were designed to look like a castle entrance.
Some newlyweds in polyester outfits were impressed.

Marcie Moran—the name was made up—was the agent
who'd handled Deborah Moore's account. Moran normally
sat at the third desk in a row of six at Your Castle, but
Karlov wanted discretion, so he interviewed her at home, a
rent-stabilized apartment in an older section of Forest Hills.
The apartment was littered with listings—little sheets of
paper indicating what was available, when, and for what
extortionist price. It was also littered with ad copy, for

Marcie Moran wrote the ads for Your Castle, the kind of blurbs that begin with FABULOUS FOUR or MUST SELL or IMPOSSIBLE! Marcie Moran could sell a condemned bomb shelter. She once did: BASEMENT BEAUTY.

She was in her fifties, appropriately slim, with a glued-on smile that could withstand a jet blast. Even the teeth had been straightened and shined for her career in Queens real estate. "A pebble's throw from Manhattan and still affordable," as she liked to say twenty to thirty times each day. She was dressed in pink slacks with matching blouse. Karlov had not told her in advance the reason for his visit, and she assumed it had something to do with a client who'd defaulted on his mortgage or wrecked an apartment.

"Do you know this person?" Karlov asked, showing Moran a picture of Deborah Moore.

Moran studied it. "She's cute," she replied.

"Was," Karlov said.

"Oh. No, I don't know her."

"You contacted her about an apartment in Queens." He had come across a letter in Deborah's files.

"I did?"

"She advertised in the paper . . ."

"Oh, well, sure, when they advertise I contact them. I try to show them the advantages of a licensed broker. Would you like to know the advantages?"

"Not right now," Karlov answered. "Does the name Deborah Moore mean anything?"

"Not immediately. I could look her up."

"She was one of the girls murdered in Manhattan—you know, by that person."

Now the smile dropped from Moran's lips. She'd never thought it was this serious. "Murdered? And *I* talked to her?"

"She lived here before moving to Manhattan. Are you sure you never brought her any customers?"

Moran waited a bit before answering. What if she *had* brought Deborah a customer? Was there one customer, a client of hers, that Karlov was investigating? It wasn't good. Real estate was reputation and referrals, and this wouldn't help.

"I want to speak with my attorney," she said.

A coldness floated over Karlov's face. What was this woman afraid of? "You can have a lawyer," he answered, "but you're not under suspicion."

Moran rethought it. No, a lawyer would make her look even worse. Better to cooperate, and maybe Karlov would leave her alone. "I don't really need a lawyer," she said. "I want to help."

"I'm surprised you didn't recognize the name," Karlov went on. "It was in the papers."

"I'm busy," Moran replied. "I read about those murders. People should live in Queens."

"Could you find out the circumstances of your contact with her?"

Moran got up and walked to a small file cabinet. In a few seconds she'd found a file on Deborah Moore. "Yes, I did speak with her," she said. "Poor girl. How could anyone ever think . . . ?"

"Do you remember her now?"

"No. There are *so* many. My notes show that I called her about her ad and asked if we could list her apartment."

"What did she say?"

"She preferred to sell it privately. You know, they want to avoid the commission. It's very foolish, because a good agent—"

"Was that the end?"

"My notes show that I visited the apartment to look it over. She allowed us to list it for a week."

"You visited, and you don't remember her?"

Moran sighed. "No, and this was only months ago. Wait, yes. I *vaguely* remember her now. She had a window in her kitchen. An important point. And . . . she wasted my time."

"Wasted your time?"

"Someone called on the phone. A repair person or something. To fix her TV. You know, someone from one of those big companies. She stayed on the phone at least five minutes. Wasted my time."

"You bring anyone up?"

"No. It wasn't a desirable apartment for my people. But I know who was up there."

"How?"

"The super. He's a friend of mine. They're *all* friends of mine. If I want to know what's happening in an apartment, they tell me."

"In exchange for—"

"I take care of my friends."

"Who was up there?"

"My notes show that almost all the people who looked at the apartment were young men. Lots of young men. Makes me wonder."

"About?"

"Young men. Was she selling the apartment or—"

"There's no evidence of that," Karlov snapped.

"Just wondering." Moran was not kind to people who didn't sell through her.

"Do your notes show any concerns of this young lady? Did she say she wanted to sell to get away from someone?"

"No."

"Was she afraid of the people coming through?"

"No. But that's a serious problem. When they don't use a broker they're at everyone's mercy. Anyone can ring that doorbell. A smart young girl always has someone with her when showing."

"Do you think the super would remember the men who visited Deborah Moore?"

"You'd have to ask him."

Karlov had one more matter to discuss with Marcie, a sensitive matter, and he had no real reason to believe she'd be helpful "Uh, one thing about real estate, ma'am."

"Yes?"

"Have you had any personnel problems in your business that I should know about—men who get into arguments with female clients?"

"In *my* firm?"

"In any."

"There are some men in other offices I wonder about."

"Any complaints?"

"I can give you their names."

"Complaints? Legal actions?"

"You'd have to check. But some of these companies, I don't think they screen their people very well."

Karlov half listened. There was a point when a witness's self-interest became such an obsession that she'd say almost anything. Marcie Moran struck him as that kind. He'd seen hundreds of them, from publicity hounds to those who thought they could profit from someone else's misfortune.

*   *   *

Karlov visited the superintendent in Deborah Moore's building, but the super couldn't recall the potential buyers who visited her. He remembered getting a complaint from one of her neighbors about too many people visiting one Saturday. Chatter in the hall. But that was the extent of it.

Karlov quizzed the neighbor, who denied complaining about Deborah once she learned that she had been murdered.

Karlov spoke with other agents. Most tried to help. Several had brought potential buyers to Deborah, and had their names and addresses. Karlov checked the agents who'd serviced the other girls, and they too had lists of potential buyers. But as Karlov checked these lists, a familiar pattern emerged: no name on one list appeared on any other. He concluded that, if the killer was using the real-estate connection, he was answering the ads directly. He wasn't going through a broker.

*   *   *

In Karlov's interviewing, one promising piece of information turned up. Karlov decided to pursue it.

There was an old man who lived across the street from Carol Krindler, the victim who'd been looking at that job offer in San Francisco. He was an invalid, and spent his days at his second-story window, just staring out at the people in the street. He volunteered to be interviewed after Carol's murder, in part because it was something exciting to do, in part because he felt he might have seen something in one of his staring sessions. He had.

Karlov walked the one flight of stairs inside the brownstone and knocked on Leon Gorshak's door. The old man wheeled himself over and opened. His face was lined, his hair was all gone, but Gorshak appeared a sprightly eighty, not allowing his infirmity to stop his life.

"You're the detective," Gorshak said in a firm voice that hadn't weakened with age.

"Karlov."

"Yeah," Gorshak said. "One of your friends was here."

"Detective Kelly."

"Yeah. That's why you're here?"

"That's right. You may have something."

"Yeah. Come on in. Excuse the smell."

Karlov had noticed that the small, dark apartment did smell like a pharmacy.

"Vaporizer," Gorshak explained, pointing to a small device emitting vapors at the side of the room, "with medicine for my throat. You get old, it happens."

"Sure," Karlov said, as Gorshak wheeled opposite a worn easy chair and gestured for Karlov to be seated. "So, you wanna know about the car."

"I sure do—exactly what you told the other detective."

"A red Ford. I seen it maybe, oh, two or three times before that girl got murdered. Now, you ask how I remember."

"I'd want to know that."

"Well," Gorshak replied, "I live at that there window. Y'see? And you get to know the cars in the neighborhood pretty well, and who drives them and what kids get in the back seat. Kids sit in the back seat, y'see."

"Sure."

"And when you get a car that comes by a couple times, real slow, you notice. Especially when it's not from around here."

"You sure it wasn't from around here?"

"Positive. Hadn't seen it before or since. A red Ford. I know it was a Ford because you get to know cars. Pretty nice car."

"Did you notice the driver?"

"He had one of those shady windows."

"Tinted?"

"Yeah, with green. It was hard to look in, and the angle isn't right from up here. It was a white guy. Besides that, I don't know."

"Did you get some idea of why he was traveling so slow?"

"It was always right past the building across the street, where the girl was. Y'know?"

"Yes."

"So I thought he was lookin' at the building. One time he actually stopped. People behind him honked."

"He always came during the day?"

"Once he came at night."

"Could you identify this car again?"

"Well," Gorshak replied, "there's a lot of red Fords out there. I could look at a car and say, 'It's like that,' but I didn't get the license or nothing'."

"Did the car have any damage?"

"Not that I noticed."

"You've been very helpful, Mr. Gorshak."

Gorshak smiled. "Yeah? Good. I'll tell Mrs. Gorshak you said so."

"Is she here?"

Gorshak laughed. "Is she *here?* She hasn't been here in a while. We're divorced, but we talk."

For the moment, Karlov was at a loss for words.

"You don't think of old people bein' divorced, do you?" Gorshak asked. "Well, we got divorced fifty-one years ago—celebrated our golden divorce anniversary last year. Still stay in touch."

"Give her my regards."

"She's a bitch."

*   *   *

Someone else had seen a red car pass Marie Gould's building before *she* was killed. It was a doorman in a building across the street, the serious kind of doorman who actually noticed everything that happened on his watch. He echoed the pattern that Gorshak had described—a car that came several times during the day, once at night, and slowed in front of the victim's building. But he couldn't say whether it was a Ford or not because he wasn't much on cars.

He had seen the driver, but not the driver's face, for the man was always looking toward Marie's building. And he hadn't caught either the license plate or any unusual features on the car. Karlov knew, of course, that this red car might not be the same red car that Leon Gorshak had seen. But the similarity in the stories had to be taken seriously.

Leonard Karlov alerted all police units in west Manhattan to be on the watch for a red car, probably a Ford, especially if it cruised slowly by apartment buildings that had no doormen.

At least it was a shot.

Finally.

The repairman paused for an instant just outside Laura Barnett's building. He checked his watch—half a minute before three o'clock. He'd called ahead to make sure Laura could keep the appointment, so he knew she'd be there. His heart trembled. Never, on one of these visits, had he felt such anticipation. There *was* something about her, something about her voice and manner, that separated her from the others.

A man left the building and the repairman turned away, so his face would not be seen. Then, using a tissue wrapped around his fingertip to avoid leaving a print, he pressed the button for Laura's apartment.

Laura answered quickly. "Yes?"

"Fred Masters."

"Oh, yes."

Laura pressed the buzzer and held it, unlocking the

building's door. The repairman entered and went straight for the elevator. As he waited for the car to come, he assessed himself in a full-length mirror. Although it was warm, he was wearing a suit and tie. It was important to look respectable, businesslike, the kind of person anyone would trust. He'd even gotten a haircut.

The elevator descended to the lobby floor and once again he turned away, so his face would not be noticed when the door opened. He entered the car, pressed the button for Laura's floor and rode up. Moments later he was standing outside her door, a door recently repainted to make the entryway as neat and appealing as possible. Again using the tissue, he rang her doorbell, then rubbed his right ear.

She opened. She looked terrific—a maroon dress and a necklace of coral beads. She had a beaming smile, a warm welcome that was meant for Fred Masters, potential buyer. The repairman convinced himself it was meant for him.

"Hi," she said. "Laura Barnett."

"Pleased," the repairman replied. He looked over her shoulder and saw trouble waiting. Glen, passive, still sitting, gazing over at the visitor, was not what he wanted to see on this balmy Saturday afternoon.

The repairman walked in. "Hello," he said to Glen.

"Hi," Glen replied, expressionless. He was still unhappy that his weekend with Laura was being interrupted by a looker.

"Are you looking, too?" the repairman asked.

"No," Laura interjected, "he's just a friend."

"Oh." Laura wasn't wearing her engagement ring— she didn't like to flaunt it—but the repairman still wondered about the "just a friend." He didn't like this friend, this *male* friend who cramped his style and intruded on his turf. This man had no *right* to be there.

"Would you like to see the apartment?" Laura asked.

"Sure."

"Okay. Well, of course this is the little foyer and that's the living room."

"I see. Oh, what a nice watch." The repairman walked over to a table and gazed down at a watch, still displayed in its box, with wrapping paper folded neatly beside it.

"Thank you," Laura said. "I kind of like it."

That made the repairman happy, since he'd sent it, its arrival designed to coincide with his. It was a Concord—not cheap and Laura knew it. He could imagine the turmoil going through her, the wondering about who would send something so expensive.

"It's nice to get gifts like that," the repairman went on. "Whoever gave it to you obviously thinks you're special."

"Why, thank you."

Glen thought this an odd observation for an apartment-hunter to make, but oddity in New York didn't provoke panic.

"Why don't we go on," Laura suggested.

"Sure."

"Please notice the wood floors in the living room. That's the original wood and I had it refinished. Also, the bookcases stay. They're built-ins."

"Lovely."

"We have a cable TV hookup."

"Uh huh. You get a good picture?"

"Yeah—and you can watch all the pornography." Laura laughed.

The repairman took out a pad and pencil and began to take notes. But his thoughts were of Laura. This was the kind of girl he'd always liked, but also the kind who'd always ignored him or turned him down.

He remained angry that Glen was there. Why should there be any competition? But he convinced himself that Glen could be overcome—especially once Laura knew who'd been sending her those terrific gifts. She'd see who was superior. She'd see the opportunity she'd been missing.

Laura began leading him into the bedroom. At that point Glen got up and joined them, not saying a word, acting as a kind of chaperone. It looked absolutely ridiculous, the repairman thought, and Laura privately thought the same. She actually felt embarrassed that Glen was trailing along.

"This is the bedroom," she said, belaboring the obvious in the same way that all people do when showing their homes. Then she noticed that her guest was looking at *her* rather than the room. "Did you have a question, Mr. Masters?"

"Uh, yes," the repairman replied, realizing he'd been caught. "I was wondering if there was any noise from upstairs when you sleep—you know, people walking around on wooden floors."

"No, actually an older lady lives up there and she's very quiet."

"I see."

Glen intervened. "Laura tells me you're moving to New York," he said.

"Yes, that's right."

"From where?"

"Chicago. I'm starting a consulting business here in computers—company executives who want to learn a lot about them fast. I'll set up courses."

"Interesting," Glen replied.

"I think so." The repairman tried desperately to avoid antagonism in his voice. But why didn't Glen go out for a beer?

"What do you think of the Apple Macintosh?" Glen suddenly asked.

Smartass, the repairman thought. Trying to show what he knew about computers. Trying to get between Laura and her new friend. "I like it," he replied. "It gets you into computing without a hassle."

"That's what I thought."

Yeah, sure, the repairman mused. He probably read it in *Consumer Reports*. "Uh, are you into computers?" he asked, at least trying to be civil.

"No, I'm a lawyer."

Ah, another one. The repairman was sure that if he drove his Ford down any Manhattan sidewalk, half the people he'd hit would be lawyers.

"A nice view out here," he said, looking out the bedroom window. "A lot of activity."

"We like that," Laura said. "That's New York."

The repairman took more notes. "Sorry about the notes," he said, "but you see so many apartments, you want to remember."

"I do the same thing," Laura answered. The repairman wondered what Laura would have said had she known that his note pad was kept next to his wallet—the wallet with her pictures in it. Maybe she would have loved it. Just maybe.

They walked into the kitchen. "I don't know how much interest you have in this," Laura said, "but we have all new appliances."

"I cook," the repairman answered, eyeing Glen, who stayed glued to Laura's side. "And I like a window in the kitchen. I see you've got one." He looked out the window, then went back and studied the dishwasher, making a note. He even leaned over to look *behind* the dishwasher and the refrigerator. "Just checking for any leakage back here," he explained.

"There's none," Glen said abruptly.

They adjourned to the living room. "Well, it's a very nice apartment," the repairman said. "Of course, I don't know that much about the neighborhood..."

"You ought to walk around," Laura suggested, sitting down. "It's a great area. We've got all kinds of people here. I mean, it's still the old city."

"I don't follow that."

"We've got *real* people in the neighborhood. We've still got the old stores, where the owners have been running them for thirty years. You can't beat that."

"I hope they stay."

"So do I."

"And it's a safe neighborhood?"

"Sure, as long as you have common sense. I mean, it *is* Manhattan and I wouldn't go walking around at three A.M. with a wad of money."

"I guess not."

"But if you use your head, nothing ever happens."

Glen broke in. "Unless that guy gets you."

"Guy?" the repairman asked.

Glen laughed, a little embarrassed at having brought it up. "Well, you know," he answered, "Mr. Mass Elimination."

"Oh, that guy who kills women," the repairman said.

"Yeah."

"I don't qualify as a victim."

"Well, *I* do," Laura said, "and I hope they catch him soon."

It was terrific, the repairman thought. Now, *this* was a trip. Here was this "friend" of wonderful Laura, this jerk standing right next to the serial killer and joking about him. The repairman almost *wanted* Glen to find out the truth, just so he could see the expression on Glen's face. And if he takes Laura away from Glen? Glen would pine his life away not even knowing that his girlfriend had been stolen by a mass murderer.

This was the top. This moment was a *thrill*.

Glen saw that the conversation was drifting. "Now, about the apartment," he said.

"Sure, the apartment," the repairman answered. "Well, it certainly is worth considering. Look, let me think about it. There are some other things I'd like to see, but this is a possibility."

"Well, any questions," Laura volunteered, "just call. We haven't, uh—"

"Discussed price."

"Yes," Laura said.

"I never discuss price unless I'm sure I want it. I know the range. I wouldn't waste your time, believe me."

The repairman looked around once more, studying every aspect of the apartment, wondering if Glen was the kind of permanent fixture who would frustrate his plans for Laura. He also began to worry about the chance of being recognized when he returned—despite the changes he'd make to his appearance. After all, it *had* almost happened with one of the other girls, and he'd had to respond by killing quickly. He operated on the belief that these women saw so many prospects come through that they never remembered the faces. But he sensed, correctly, that Laura hadn't had that many bites. This one might be more difficult.

He started walking toward the front door, Laura accompanying him. "I'll be in touch," he said.

"I hope so," Laura answered. "I really do."

The repairman left the apartment. Oh, would he ever be in touch. If only Laura realized what she'd been requesting, what she'd been *inviting*. In touch. *So* in touch.

He rode down in the elevator and left quickly, walking out onto the hot sidewalk. But he stepped out into the street for a moment and looked back, examining the building. He knew Laura might be at her window, and he wanted to show interest in the place, as any prospective buyer might. It made him more legitimate, more serious. Then he walked toward the red Ford, parked more than three blocks away. In his pocket: the note pad, with the valuable information, the critical information that would make the next step in his plan possible.

* * *

"Terrific," Glen said, mildly disgusted as he slumped into a living room chair. "*That* was a live one?"

"Maybe he is," Laura replied.

"He was a looker," Glen retorted. "We've wasted an entire day here while he looked."

"How can you be so sure?"

"Instinct. And I *don't* think he's from out of town. I think he lives right here."

"Why?"

"Out-of-towners come with agents."

"Well, maybe he's different."

"I think we should restrict this apartment-showing to one day on each weekend," Glen said, knowing that Laura had scheduled three other appointments the next day.

"All right. But we want to sell it before the wedding."

"We'll sell it," Glen said, "but not to him. You'll never see *him* again."

He walked to the window and looked out at the strolling crowds. The red Ford drove past, but Glen didn't notice it.

Laura did think she'd see Fred Masters again. Her instinct told her he was interested. He'd looked around more carefully than most. He'd asked the right questions. He hadn't just rushed through. She barely got a chance to look at his face—she was too busy showing him all the apartment details—but she *liked* him. He had a courteous, gentle manner. She hoped he'd come back. He'd be a pleasure, she thought, to do business with.

The *New York Register* had more ads than any other paper in the region, and its real-estate section was probably the most complete in the country. If you wanted to sell a house or apartment, this was your first call—the three-line ads, arranged by type of residence and location, as in HOUSES-WESTCHESTER. There were people in New York who read the ads because they were buying, selling, curious about how much their residence might be worth, or equally curious about whether an ad was from their neighbor, and why. Real estate was big business in a town where apartments could go for a million dollars, give or take two or three hundred thousand, and houses for $250,000 in some areas were considered bottom end.

Leonard Karlov walked in the revolving front door, showed his ID to a guard, and took the elevator to the floor where ad takers worked the phones, receiving ad copy all day long. Karlov's visit stemmed from the one solid idea

167

he'd picked up from Marcie Moran: if the victims had wanted to avoid real-estate brokers, their main contact with buyers would have been through classified ads.

Seymour Merson ran the ad department, and ran it the way an old-school captain ran a great ocean liner of the 1930s. To Merson, this was major journalism. Ads were the backbone of the paper, the commerce that produced the news pages and the special sections. *He* was responsible, and on his shoulders rested the future of the publication and, one would imagine from his demeanor, the future of all humankind.

He was of medium height, with a thick mustache and a haircut done at Bergdorf's. He'd even had the carpeting in his office changed from gray to red because a survey showed that red meant an important executive worked there.

"We're here to help you," he told Karlov as the detective entered his office. But Merson didn't get up. An executive remained seated. "As journalists, we feel a responsibility."

"Thanks," Karlov said. He hadn't been asked to sit down, but did anyway, in a fairly plush visitors' chair of dark brown. He looked up on the wall and saw a number of awards for ad revenue, each one in a silver frame.

"Battle ribbons," Merson said.

"Very impressive."

"We try.'

"I need some information."

"Shoot."

"It'll be difficult, but we want to know the names of young, single women who've placed apartment ads."

"Why?"

"For an investigation."

"The serial killer."

"Well, that's right. It's hard to hide it, but I wouldn't want it discussed. We don't want to scare people with theories that may turn out to be wrong."

"You're asking a lot," Merson retorted. "As journalists, we report the news. You're asking me to hold something back."

"But this is the *ad* department."

"It's a newspaper. We're all reporters, just as everyone in the Army is basically an infantryman," Merson said defensively.

Karlov knew the type. He'd dealt with screaming egos before, and knew how to work them. "I understand your problem," he said, "but this is a matter of the public interest. Lives are involved. There's really no news yet because it's all in my head. If there is, well . . . we all know who gets it first. I know the public interest has always been important here."

"Of course."

"You'd never want to be responsible for lives lost. I know I can count on you."

"Certainly."

"So I can entrust you with highly sensitive information?"

"It's done all the time," Merson said, fully willing to compromise his position as ace reporter to get some really good gossip.

"We believe," Karlov continued, "that the serial killer might be reading real-estate ads."

"And answering them?"

"Yes."

Merson shrugged. "I don't know. Women who place these ads know that any creep can answer them. We have some research on this. They usually accept visitors only in daytime, and usually with someone around."

"These may be exceptions."

"Five exceptions? That was the number, wasn't it?"

"Yes." Now Karlov was becoming irritated. It wasn't Merson's place to question the police judgment. There was a risk that Merson might turn out to be more disaster than help. "We feel strongly about this," Karlov said. "He can strike any night."

Merson understood. A delay could cost a life. "All right, young, single women who've placed apartment ads..."

"... West Side in buildings with no doormen," Karlov added.

"Tough to track."

"I've got fifty men."

"What will you do with the names?"

Karlov hesitated, moving uneasily in his chair. "I'm assuming they might be next," he said.

"Then issue a public warning—women should be careful if they're advertising."

"He'd just change tactics," Karlov replied, "and there are some realities."

Merson didn't have to ask about that. He knew the power of real-estate interests in New York City, how appalled they'd be by an announcement that real-estate transactions might involve physical risk. Karlov knew how the investigation might be tampered with, even wrecked, by political forces beholden to the builders. Since he didn't think a public warning would really do any good, why take them on?

"We have four ad takers who specialize in real-estate," Merson said. 'I'll assign someone to help you."

"I may have to visit those women," Karlov said. "I may have to warn them."

"We understand."

*   *   *

Merson took Karlov out to the action area, where ad-takers sat in rows of glass cubicles answering the phones and tapping the ad orders into computers. It was remarkably quiet, primarily because the ceilings were soundproofed and the ad-takers had learned to modulate their voices or lose them during a hectic day.

"I'm giving you my best man," Merson said, walking down an aisle lined with the cubicles. "He can tap up any data you want."

"Thanks," Karlov said.

After winding through a maze of aisles, they stopped. A man was taking an order on the phone. Karlov was impressed with his warmth, his manner, the utter professionalism with which he quoted the rates, took the information, suggested modifications. He finished his conversation and hung up.

"Detective," Merson said, "I'd like you to meet our premier ad salesman. Gordon West."

West had his back to the two men. As he turned around he reached up to his right ear and started rubbing it nervously.

27

"Gordon," Merson said, "this is Detective Karlov."

Gordon West practically felt a bolt of electricity slam through him. Karlov. He knew the name. It had been in all the papers, and on radio and TV. This guy was in charge of the investigation.

So they'd got him. He was caught. He'd surrender with dignity, with style—the doors were probably sealed anyway—and face the jury, maybe write his memoirs. He could get a lot for those.

Somehow, he'd slipped up, and now, in the seconds he had to contemplate his situation, he cursed himself. What had he done wrong? What had he overlooked?

He stared at Karlov and Karlov seemed to be staring back. West was ordinary-looking, medium height with a roundish face and smallish brown eyes. He was partially bald, with the remaining hair reddish brown and somewhat curly. He wore an inexpensive gray suit, but it was meticulously clean and freshly pressed.

"Do you want me?" he asked Karlov, already knowing the answer.

"Yes." Karlov replied.

"How did you know it was me?"

Karlov was thrown by the question, or at least its form. "Mr. Merson told me. He said you knew more about this department than anyone else, and that's what I want."

For a moment, West just stared at Karlov. What the hell was this guy talking about? "You want to know about the department?" he asked.

"I need some research in who placed what ads."

West felt the muscles inside him melt into supreme repose. Jesus! Here was the detective in charge of *his* murders, and he wasn't there to arrest him! Gordon felt almost offended. He wasn't getting the attention he deserved. Was this real? Some kind of cruelty? Was Karlov making his arrest through the back door? "I'll try to help you," he said. What else could he say?

"What I'm looking for," Karlov explained, "are the names of young, single women who've placed ads to sell apartments. I'll restrict that to women who are now living in buildings on the West Side, without doormen."

"You involved with these killings?" West asked.

"I'd rather not discuss my work."

So, West thought, there it was. Karlov had found the real-estate connection. West half expected himself to panic, but he didn't. In fact, he was finding the whole thing bizarre and almost entertaining. All right, Karlov was bright. But there was the other link—and Karlov would *never* find that one. Gordon was sure. It was the little gimmick that made it possible for him to gain easy entry to his victims' apartments, and it was brilliant. He'd stay ahead of the game, even with Karlov right next to him.

Right next to him!

If only the girls who'd turned their backs in Winnetka could see him now. No doubt about it—he was the most successful member of the class of '64.

He didn't sense it, but his hands were shaking. Karlov assumed it was only a nervous habit, but West hadn't realized how scared he'd been when Karlov was first introduced.

"We don't keep files by sex or age," West explained. "Maybe Mr. Merson told you."

"I suspected that," Karlov replied.

"But we do have the billing name and address, and many bills are to women. They could be married, but most of them are single."

"If the people who run the ads move, do you have a way of finding out?"

"Not really. We don't track our advertisers that way. But you could check with circulation. If they had a subscription, they might have had it changed."

Karlov instantly liked Gordon West. The man seemed competent and helpful.

And West liked Karlov. The detective didn't seem naturally suspicious or unduly aggressive.

"Do you get people calling and asking about the ads?" Karlov inquired.

"You mean, people asking for more information?"

"That's right."

"Sure. Especially when the ad has a box number here at the paper. You know, a reply address. People call thinking we have more information on the apartment."

"But you don't."

"We tell them to write, and the person placing the ad gets the letter."

"Did any one person call over and over, I mean in recent months?"

"I wouldn't know," West said. "I haven't heard that."

"Does the paper get any complaints about people answering these ads and acting suspicious, or unruly?"

"Not really. We get complaints about misprints. But if people complain about the respondents, they'd go to the police, I guess." He looked over at Merson. "Wouldn't you say so, Mr. Merson?"

"Sure."

"Do you ever take surveys on the effectiveness of your ads—you know, how many responses people get?"

"Certainly," Gordon replied. "We do that all the time. That's how we know how to advise our advertisers."

"So it's possible that names of your advertisers would be listed in those surveys."

"Yes. Those people are promised anonymity, though."

"I'm not publishing their names."

Merson left and Karlov conferred with Gordon West for a few minutes more. Later that afternoon he returned with twenty-three plainsclothesmen who, with Gordon's help, pored through records of past ad placements, trying to put together a list of women who'd advertised. The list, remarkably, was not that long. Most women, especially young, single women, didn't own apartments, and those who did usually remained where they were, financially unable to make a move. Karlov never told West that he was looking for the names of *potential* victims, women his department could watch, could warn, could track.

It was true that the files gave no guide to age, but Karlov could easily match names and addresses against driver's license records, which did give age. And there were other public records he could tap—business applications, permits, loan forms, birth certificates, even divorce judgments. He liked to say that there was no privacy left in America, something he feared because of his parents' background, yet something he used in his police work. It was ironic, though, that the very lack of privacy might now save some young woman's life. She would, some day, consider herself lucky that someone had probed into her affairs and put her name down on a special list.

*   *   *

It took fully three days for Karlov and his men to complete their work. Gordon West was remarkably helpful, even calling Karlov at home one night with the names of women who'd placed ads that day, and whose invoices were not yet in the files. Karlov appreciated that. Most people tried to avoid the police, or ran to their lawyer whenever a policeman called. Here was a good citizen who wanted to do his part. He also wanted to talk.

"I hope we're helping," West said, speaking from his almost dark apartment in Queens.

"You're more than helping," Karlov replied, lying in bed as he spoke. "You're above and beyond."

"I guess you think this nut answered some of our ads," West said.

Karlov wasn't annoyed by the probe. What he was doing was obvious to any thoughtful person, and West was thoughtful. "Yeah, that's one theory."

"It's a good one. But it doesn't go far enough."

"Oh?"

"I've thought about it myself," West continued, Karlov listening intently. "He may answer these ads, but some of these girls were killed months after they placed them."

"That's right."

"How do you figure that?"

"Well, I . . . I really can't discuss official business with you," Karlov replied, trying to be as polite as possible to a man he respected, "but it's a very good point."

"I mean," West went on, "he didn't kill them while replying to those ads. People don't reply months later."

"Of course not."

"I've got an idea."

"Really?"

"I think he answered their ads, then dated them. But I think he wasn't their usual stuff."

"Usual stuff?" Karlov was fascinated with West's thinking, and was self-effacing enough to listen to someone without a badge.

"He wasn't as, let's say, high-quality as the types they usually dated. So they wouldn't talk about him to their friends. Otherwise, you would've come up with the name."

Jesus, Karlov thought, the guy might have it! It fit, it was logical! A man would answer the ads—an attractive man, maybe even suave. He'd get to know the women. Maybe they'd be in a mood for a fling. He might have been unemployed, or an ex-convict, or maybe he had a menial job, or maybe there was something else that made him "unacceptable" for a long-term relationship, but fine for an affair. The women had been embarrassed. He wasn't a prestige item, so they hadn't mentioned him to friends. Or maybe he'd *asked* not to be mentioned. Maybe he'd told them he was ending a marriage and didn't want his private contacts to get back to his wife. The women might have found this intriguing, exciting. Maybe they'd even felt sorry for him.

"You're making some good points," Karlov said.

"I've thought it out," West answered. "This fellow had to be there, but anonymous at the same time. He could've even been foreign, and told these girls he was in America illegally. Don't mention my name, that sort of thing."

"Another good point."

"Well, I've known a lot of girls," West said. "You get to know how they think."

"Yeah."

"Believe me, women don't open doors to men they don't know, especially at night. Mr. Merson probably told you that."

"He did."

"That goes double for women in no-doorman buildings. We know that territory. They're all scared. There's no daddy at the front door, if you catch me."

"I do."

Gordon West was loving it. Here was the highest expression of the murderer's deception—speaking to the very man who was looking for him, and conning him. He'd do it again and again, he told himself. Lead Karlov off the track. Plant ideas in the detective's brain. Good ideas, ideas that seem to point to some solution to the serial murders.

Never, Gordon was sure, had there been this relationship between a detective and his target. And yet, Karlov would never realize it. He would go to his grave broken and frustrated by the serial killer. Gordon West felt almost sorry for him; he respected Karlov the way a general can respect a senior officer of an enemy army.

The conversation soon ended. Gordon West felt a wonderful satisfaction with his performance. He was first class. Absolutely first class. He went back to his computer and tapped up the file on Laura Barnett. He wanted to memorize everything, to be ready for the ultimate night that he knew would come.

* * *

But Karlov was disgusted with himself. *He* should have thought of those ideas. Women do have secret lives that they don't share with even their closest friends. Some travel to Europe to have these little affairs. Some carry them on at home, but discreetly.

He put through a call to Harold Kramer, who, he knew, was working late at the ME's office. The weather was warm, the nights humid, and the result was a sudden increase in homicides, mostly in neighborhoods where air conditioning was rare. Kramer got part of the autopsy overflow, certifying that so-and-so had died of a gunshot wound to the chest fired at close range. He had just finished exploring a twenty-three-year-old woman from the Lower East Side, a stabbing victim, when he was called to the phone.

"I feel like a dumb cop," Karlov began, without the usual amenities.

This had to be it, Kramer thought, still in his green surgical gown. Karlov had cracked it and was being modest. It had been something obvious all along, something that had been overlooked. "Tell me about dumb," Kramer replied.

"I was just talking to this guy from the paper. He gets a lot of these ads and he knows the kind of women who put them in. He had an idea—these women are having secret flings with this guy, the kind of guy they don't talk about."

"And they met through the ads."

"Yeah."

"Len," Kramer replied, "that is the first coherent theory the case has had."

"That's what I say."

"We've had any number of corpses in here because of these secret things. Women get involved with the wrong kind, they don't mention it, and the guy turns out to be a slasher.''

"And even if some women turn him down," Karlov went on, "he'd just answer more ads. He gets an endless supply of prospects from the newspaper."

"The house-hunter lover," Kramer said.

"You should work for the *Post*."

"If this job get any worse, I *will*."

Karlov quickly narrowed the list to single women on the West Side of Manhattan living in apartment buildings with no doorman. Some detectives wanted it restricted further, to women whose apartments, like those of the victims, had only one bedroom. But Karlov thought the size of the apartment was probably coincidence, and refused to narrow the list.

It was easy for him to deduce why the killer chose buildings with no doormen—there was no one in the lobby to remember him. But he wondered why he never struck isolated suburban homes. Karlov concluded that few single women lived in those homes, and that the killer feared he might be spotted in a low-density suburban area. In the city he just melted into the crowd.

Karlov's final list had only eighteen names. He knew that any one might be the next target. One might already have been killed, her body waiting to be discovered. He also knew his plan might be off base, with the murderer preparing to strike somewhere else. As a first precaution, though, he had his detectives phone each name on the list, stating that the department was cautioning women against meeting men at home, or opening their doors to men they didn't know thoroughly.

Then, detectives started visiting each woman on the list. Karlov had his own names. Among them was Laura Barnett.

*   *   *

Laura wasn't surprised by Karlov's visit. She had, after all, filed a complaint about the anonymous gifts and assumed that was why she was picked to be interviewed. But she could not take seriously the idea that she could be a victim of the serial killer. She was normally with Glen, no one else was asking to see her, and she'd never open her door to anyone but Glen.

In fact, once Karlov learned that Laura was engaged, he thought the interview with her might be unproductive. Why would the killer waste his time on an engaged woman? And if the "fling" theory was correct, it wouldn't apply to a woman who'd just decided to get married. But he visited her anyway, on a night when Glen wasn't there. Indeed, Laura had asked that the interview be scheduled on one of Glen's working nights so it wouldn't conflict with her time with him. Karlov showed up with a standard list of questions he'd drawn up for his men, as well as some specialized questions for Laura alone.

He was immediately taken with Laura—the bright smile, the large eyes, and yet the fierce independence those eyes clearly showed. Laura Barnett seemed unafraid, unrattled by the presence of a detective investigating the most savage crimes against women the city had seen in years.

But Laura was instantly less impressed with Karlov than she'd been with Detective Beer. Beer may have been pompous, but he had style, he was sharp, he was well dressed, he exuded success. Karlov was plodding, methodical but hardly overflowing with flair, and his thinnish, sad face didn't project that bulldog image a detective was supposed to have. Laura didn't let her first impression show, however, as Karlov sat down and began his interview.

"Uh, Miss Barnett, or do you prefer Ms.?"

"Ms.," Laura replied. "Even after I'm married."

"Certainly. I'm here, Ms. Barnett, because of this fellow who's been killing women."

"Yes, I understand."

"I also see in my file that you've registered a complaint with the department."

"Detective Beer."

"Right. Beer. I know him. You were bothered by gifts that came anonymously. You complained about a former male friend, is that right?"

"Well, I didn't *complain*. I thought it might be him."

"And the department surveilled him and found nothing. Have the gifts continued?"

"I got a sterling silver pen."

"Very baffling," Karlov said. "But I don't relate it to the serial murderer."

"Well, that's good."

"Our concern, Ms. Barnett, is with women like yourself who've been victimized. I want to caution you about allowing anyone in the apartment who shouldn't be here."

"I'm very careful about that."

"Have you seen anyone watching the building?"

"No."

"Have other women you know complained about particular men?"

"Well," Laura replied, "women always have complaints about some men. But I've heard nothing involving violence."

"Have any friends noticed that men they know weren't available the nights of these murders?"

"That's a good one," Laura answered. "No one's brought it up."

"Ma'am, you've advertised in the paper."

"Yes, for my apartment."

"Any callers?"

"Sure."

"Young men? Men who might find you attractive?"

Laura blushed. "Well, I don't know if they . . . yes, there were some young men."

"Did it appear that some really weren't interested in the apartment? I mean, did they appear to come for some other purpose?"

Laura thought for a moment. "I think they were all interested. But, it's really hard to say. Most people are just lookers, but try to appear interested. Or some just don't like the place, and that's that. I couldn't really make an absolute judgment."

She was thoughtful, Karlov realized. He felt sure she was giving him accurate answers.

"Did any of them leave immediately after seeing your fiance, Mr. . . . ?"

"Glen?"

"Yes. I had it written down."

"Well," Laura shrugged. "I don't think it was *because*

of Glen. One left fast, but I think he wanted a larger apartment.''

"How about phone calls, ma'am?'' Karlov asked. "Did any of these men call you back and try to get into conversations?''

"No,'' Laura sighed, "we haven't had a single call-back yet. We're not making a big hit with the apartment crowd.''

"I'm sure you'll be successful, ma'am. I wish you'd try to recall if there were any unusual incidents since you placed your ad.''

"I'll try,'' Laura promised, "but I honestly don't think there was anything . . .''

She stopped. Karlov thought he saw a curious expression in her eyes. "Yes, what is it?'' he asked.

"Oh, nothing.''

"Please!''

Laura took in a breath and let it out slowly. "Well, *I* didn't think this was unusual, but Glen . . . he's a lawyer.''

"What did Glen see?''

"There was a very nice fellow who came up.''

"Name?''

"A Fred Masters.''

"And what did Glen find unusual about Masters?''

"Well, just that he said he was from out of town and came up without an agent. Glen thought that was unusual. I didn't.''

"Aside from that, anything about him suspicious?'' Karlov asked.

"No.''

"Has he called back?''

"No, not yet. I wish he would.''

"Doesn't sound like much to me,'' Karlov concluded.

"Maybe he didn't like real-estate agents, or thought he could make a better deal without one."

"Sure. I agree," Laura said. "But I just thought I'd mention it."

"I'm glad you did. But look," Karlov said, "I wish you'd call me if you suspect anything at all. Trust your instincts. That's the first lesson in crime prevention. If you think something's wrong, it probably is. Let me tell you an interesting statistic. About eighty percent of the women who think their husbands are having an affair turn out to be right. Isn't that incredible?"

"Yes," Laura answered, squirming with some embarrassment. It was not a statistic to delight a soon-to-be bride.

"And all of them find out by following their instincts," Karlov went on.

"I'll call you if I suspect something," Laura promised.

"But first I've got some more questions," Karlov said. "However, I'm afraid they're . . . sensitive."

"Sensitive?"

"I may have to ask you about your past social life. There may be . . . personal matters."

"Well, I . . . guess that would be all right," Laura said, realizing she might be asked things she wouldn't even reveal to Glen and relieved, in a way, that he wasn't there.

"If there's something you honestly don't want to answer, tell me," Karlov requested.

"Oh, I will, believe me. But . . . shoot."

Karlov gazed into Laura's eyes. They were inquisitive now, but fearful, as if wondering what challenge was about to descend, what intimate details would be probed.

And Laura's mind raced as she waited for Karlov's questions and pondered the possibilities. Maybe he'd asked about Jason. That would be logical. But maybe he'd also ask about *Glen*. Could he be thinking that Glen...? No, Glen had been with her on several of the murder nights. But Karlov didn't know that yet, did he?

This was getting serious. Laura felt a sudden tension she hadn't experienced when Karlov first arrived. She almost felt she was being clinically examined.

"Relax, ma'am," Karlov said, realizing her discomfort. "You're not suspected of anything, and I'll try to make this as quick as possible."

"Thank you."

"I'm wondering whether you've had, uh, social experiences with men recently who you didn't talk about."

"I've been with Glen, only Glen."

"No casual relationships on the side, even ones that were ending?"

"No."

"Before meeting Glen, did you have any relationships with men who you found, oh, embarrassing?"

"Embarrassing?"

"You know, you found them attractive in one way, but you wouldn't want to bring them home."

"I see what you mean. Purely physical things."

"In general, yes, ma'am."

"No, I can't admit to that kind of excitement," Laura said. "I've discussed every man I've dated with my friends."

"Have there been any men—rough men maybe—who've tried to solicit such a relationship?"

"No. I'm old-fashioned. I know what can happen with bad relationships. That's the story with the man I complained about to Detective Beer."

"Jason Hebert."

"Yes."

"Ma'am, I apologize in advance for this, but have you ever used a male escort service?"

"Absolutely not!"

"Okay, okay. I just had to ask it. Have you ever befriended a vagrant, or a lonely old man in the park, someone you'd open the door to?"

Laura thought for a few moments. Karlov watched her eyes and realized he'd struck something. "No vagrants," Laura said.

"I'm again talking about the kind of person you might not mention."

"Well, I do walk in the park, mostly with Glen. But sometimes, on a weekend, if he's got to see a client, I go to a small playground near here to watch the children play. There's an old man there, Al."

"Just Al?"

"I don't know his last name. Everyone calls him Al. He just sits there all day and gives candy to the kids. He lives a block away."

"You consider him a friend?"

"Not really, but he always comes over to me. He once rang the buzzer downstairs. It was a rainy day and he didn't want to walk home. I think he was just lonely. I think he's *always* lonely. So I let him in and gave him hot chocolate."

"Did he come again?"

"No. Never."

"Did he say or do anything improper?"

"Al? He's not the type."

"They never are, ma'am." Karlov wrote down all the information. "Could you give me the gentlemen's address?"

"I don't know the number," Laura replied. "It's one street north, a white brick building in the middle of the block. He once told me he was on the fourth floor, and that he was a retired dress salesman."

"I'll check it out."

"Look, you don't think that Al . . . ?"

"Not really. But we look into everything."

"Al is just a gentle old man. He's got to be eighty. He couldn't hurt anyone."

"Probably not. Now, I'd like to ask you about this Jason Hebert. I know you've discussed him with Detective Beer."

"Yes."

"People reading your file would think he's a rather unusual sort for someone like you."

"Yes, he is. But people fall into these things."

"That's why I was wondering whether there's someone else like that."

"What do you mean?"

"Well, I think you're a little embarrassed by this Jason."

"Who wouldn't be?"

"And maybe there's been someone else like that, and you're blocking him out."

"I can't blame you for thinking that," Laura replied, "but there really isn't."

Karlov completed his questioning. What continued to strike him about Laura was her attractiveness. It worried him, because the serial killer would almost certainly be taken by her if he came into contact . . . and he might come into contact through her apartment ad. He got the feeling that Laura wasn't naturally suspicious, and, despite her precautions, would be off guard against a resourceful killer.

"I want to stress again," he told her, "how dangerous this man is."

"Oh, I understand that," Laura replied.

"Even so, I get the sense that you feel it can't happen to you. Ma'am, that very dangerous."

Somehow, Karlov's last statement hit home. Emotionally, Laura still didn't believe it could happen to her. It was a natural outgrowth of having Glen, and of having handled Jason in the past. "I'll be careful," she told Karlov. "It *can* happen to me. Your coming made that clear."

"Again, please call me on anything you think important," Karlov said. "And tell your friends to do the same. If you know any women who are placing real-estate ads, I'd like their names, too—for their protection."

"Of course. Should I continue showing the apartment?" Laura asked.

"As long as your fiance is with you," Karlov replied. "At no other time."

*   *   *

He left a few minutes later, and he left Laura far more affected by the presence of the serial killer than she'd been before. She realized she'd been so glib about it, so New York—sure of her own security. Her emotions now began to budge, now that she was alone, that someone wasn't there to protect her. It *could* happen, couldn't it? Some unguarded moment. Some slip. Maybe she'd forgotten something, or someone. Maybe she could be a victim, perhaps the next victim. But why? There were so many other women who weren't engaged. Wouldn't the killer try to get one of *them?* And Laura began to fear for *all* the women in her neighborhood. There were so many conflicts in her feelings—feelings of safety combined with vulnerability, feelings that all this wasn't real, and feelings that she just couldn't accept the reality.

She couldn't wait for Glen to arrive. She needed him more than ever.

*   *   *

Gordon West saw Karlov leave Laura's building.

He saw him from the shadows, half a block away. He saw him get into his car and drive off.

And he knew Laura was alone.

He had his camera, loaded with superfast film. He wanted a picture of her at the window, maybe in a nightgown, maybe in less, maybe getting ready for bed.

And yet, he also felt the urge to abandon his tactics, do something dramatic, dashing, manly.

Go see her, he told himself.

Get into the building somehow and go to her. Charm her. Sweep her off her feet.

His insides burned and his heart pounded like some giant pump. God, why not? Why not *get* there before this other man got there?

He felt in his pocket for the sharpened screwdriver he carried for protection. If she resisted, if she turned out to be foolish like the others, he would take care of her with his powerful, single thrust. He always had that option, that power. And he knew he'd then forget her, just as he'd forgotten all of them. And he'd leave two glasses of Coke, so the police would know that Laura Barnett had been killed by a friend.

But she wouldn't resist.

He *knew* that.

He'd felt that magic when he looked through her apartment, and he sensed she'd felt it too.

He started walking out of the shadows, toward the building.

Walking closer.

Closer.

He was thirty yards from the door.

And then he saw Glen coming up the street.

Gordon slipped back into the shadows.

Fate. Fate was cursing him. Why did this jerk have to come along at *this* time?

He hated Glen. He wanted to rush out and kill him, keeping him from Laura forever.

But he didn't, for Gordon West was afraid that in a violent encounter with a man, he'd lose. And he couldn't take the humiliation.

29

Karlov felt he'd done all he could to protect potential victims. He was in constant touch with Gordon West at the paper, getting the names of new advertisers, and contacting them in turn. No new clues turned up, and Karlov still feared that this one might never be solved. He also knew the killer might stop for a time, then resume, or that someone else might copy him, or appear to copy him.

The situation was difficult enough, but, in line with the logic of these things, it suddenly got much worse when Karlov picked up a copy of the *New York Post* and took one look at the front page: THE APARTMENT-HUNTING KILLER.

Someone had leaked, and to a competing paper. It wasn't long before Karlov, working through his contacts in the press, learned that the leaker was Seymour Merson, Gordon West's boss, who had pledged secrecy in the public interest. Merson apparently wanted his moment of glory, perhaps offered the tip to his own paper and was turned down, then offered it to the *Post*. Karlov resolved never to let Merson know he'd been found out, but also resolved that someday, somewhere, Merson wouldn't find a friend in the police department when he needed one.

So it was out. The real-estate connection had been released, and soon it was in every paper and on all the local news shows, and Karlov realized that whatever chance he had might have gone down the drain. The reporters started calling, and he had no choice but to confirm the accuracy of the *Post*'s story. Yes, he had concluded that the killer had met his victims through ads. Yes, he had wanted to keep it secret, but he understood the *Post*'s position—news was news. He'd learned long ago that it was never a good idea to get angry at the press.

Karlov had to assume that the killer, if he continued, would change his tactics. Or would he? Maybe he'd go right on doing the same thing because it wouldn't be expected of him.

Ironically, the premature release boosted Karlov's stock substantially. Both inside and outside the department there was recognition of the dogged investigating and attention to detail he had brought to the case. Brooklyn wasn't very impressed, of course. The Brooklyn DA charged that "police data" had been incorrectly leaked to newspapers. He further suggested that "it would appear that some officer, perhaps seeking publicity," might have been at fault. But that was the only accusing finger wagged at Leonard Karlov, although he knew there'd be handfuls if the killings went on.

*   *   *

Laura and Glen read the latest headlines with utter fascination. Karlov had been right. In a way, they felt a degree of protection and security they'd not felt since the start of the anonymous gifts and the beginning of the serial murders. "Forewarned is forearmed," Glen kept saying, repeating a cliché that Laura had never particularly liked.

They could concentrate on more important things, like the wording of the engagement announcement they now planned to put in the paper. It was time, they felt, and, besides, Glen had to go on a short business trip and wanted to get the announcement out of the way.

As always, they spent their early evenings in Laura's apartment, this time with pads and pencils. They knew their friends and relatives would read the announcement, and wanted to be sure no one was offended, or even surprised. Engagement announcements were diplomatic documents, properly arranged with all the care of a peace treaty.

"Tradition is the best way," Laura said one evening. "Everyone understands, and no one gets miffed."

"Affirmed," Glen replied. "But I don't want to make it look like we're a bunch of society jerks. You know, 'the Barnetts of someplace and somewhere happily announce...'"

"So we'll keep it informal," Laura said. "What about, 'Hey, look who's gettin' married?'"

They both laughed—the first good laugh they'd had in a long time.

"We haven't discused the trip," Glen said, putting down his pencil for a moment. And it was true, they both wanted a honeymoon trip, but had given it very little thought.

"Let's see how much money we have first," Laura suggested. "I hate to plan and be disappointed." She still concentrated on the announcement. "Why not simply, 'Mr. and Mrs. Ralph Barnett...'"

"Europe," Glen said.

"Glen, let's get this written."

"California? Hawaii?"

"Glen, there's an announcement to be written."

"Staten Island. We'll do it cheap."

"That's the best idea you've had. Now, 'Mr. and Mrs. Ralph Barnett happily . . . ' No, Let's leave out the *happily*. You're right, it sounds too stodgy. 'Mr. and Mrs. Ralph Barnett announce the engagement of their daughter, Laura Ann . . . ' "

"Oh Jesus," Glen complained.

"You don't like the full name?"

"What is it, a birth certificate? That's why these things all sound so puffed up. Just Laura."

"I *like* Laura Ann."

"Well, it's your name, so I guess you win. But don't call me Glen Franklin please. I could never stand that, and I don't want us to sound like a gang of yuppies."

"In a way, we are."

"No, we're not," Glen replied, and Laura could see that he was deadly serious. "Yuppies wouldn't start out in the U.S. attorney's office. There's not enough money in it."

Laura liked that. Glen still had that spark of idealism. "You're right," she said, "we're not."

They struggled through the wording of the announcement, finally coming up with something not too different from the traditional one that Laura wanted.

* * *

Karlov planned the next phase of his investigation by concentrating on one tactic he'd not yet used: perhaps he could lure the killer into coming to *him*. It would work only if the murderer continued using real-estate ads, and Karlov rated the chances of that at no better than fifty-fifty. But it was worth a try. He called Lieutenant Sheila McBride, one of the highest-ranking women in homicide, to his office.

He'd worked with McBride before, and realized she had a superb organizational ability—precisely what was needed at the moment.

McBride appeared in his office in civilian clothes, a gray business suit with light blue blouse. She was smallish, with close-cropped hair that stood out because of its bright red color. She'd worn glasses for years, but now had new contacts that were still giving her trouble. Her left eye blinked more than it should, and she apologized to Karlov at the start. McBride had done some field work on the serial murder case, warning possible victims and checking out anonymous tips. She didn't have to be briefed on the situation.

"Sheila," Karlov said, leaning back in his chair and trying to seem as relaxed as possible, "the way it stands right now, we're waiting for the next woman to get stabbed in the chest."

McBride just nodded, her usual response.

"I think," Karlov went on, "we've got to bring that guy to us. We've got to smoke him out."

"How?"

"*If* he'll still respond to apartment ads, and it's a gigantic if, we've got to create our own set of victims."

"Policewomen."

"Yes. The idea is for your people to place ads in the paper and wait for responses."

"Wait where?"

"I could get some real-estate people to cooperate. There are still some empty apartments in Manhattan. We could put in furniture and set the women up. Of course, they'd be fully protected. If they wanted to use their own apartments, that would be all right, too."

"If he's still answering ads, what are the chances he'll be smoked out?"

"Good, I think. The ads run by the victims all had things in common—the size of the apartment, location, a certain price range, the type of building. We could duplicate those ads. Your policewomen would take callers the way anyone would who's selling or subletting."

"Why do my people have to place the ads? Why don't we just write a bunch of ads and bring them in?"

"No way," Karlov replied. "We've already had a massive leak from those SOBs. I want these ads called in the way you'd call in any ads. The paper will not be told what we're doing."

"When do I start?"

"Now."

"I'll get a group. How many?"

"About twelve women."

"I'll check with you on the ad copy," Sheila said.

"Okay."

And that was that—the typical McBride efficiency. Within twenty-four hours she'd handpicked twelve women who, she thought, could make convincing phone calls to a paper, place ads, then show an apartment as if they'd really wanted to sell it. She returned to Karlov with twelve different ads, each one appropriate to the mission.

"I suggest some of the women show concern over the killer when they call the paper," McBride told Karlov.

"Excellent idea."

"A few should say that they were warned by relatives about selling now, but that they know how to be careful—that kind of thing."

"But they shouldn't sound rehearsed," Karlov cautioned.

"They *are* rehearsed," McBride replied. "Part of their rehearsal is not to sound rehearsed."

Karlov knew he'd picked precisely the right person.

The women started making their calls, and Karlov once

again got in touch with Gordon West at the paper. He saw the policewomen's calls starting to show up in West's reports. Karlov made sure to have the calls carefully spaced so that they weren't all made within a few days.

Some of the policewomen were set up in apartments provided by Karlov's contacts in real estate—real-estate people loved to do favors for the police, who could do favors for them in return. But most of the women chose to use their own apartments. All the policewomen were single.

The women started getting replies, most of them completely legitimate, a few from obvious cranks responding to the publicity about the real-estate connection, making obscene remarks and hanging up. Karlov had expected that.

30

Gordon West couldn't believe it. It was the ultimate betrayal, the final slap in the face. "Mr. and Mrs.
Ralph Barnett announce . . ."

Gordon read it at breakfast, in his own paper. He
always read the engagement announcements, his only contact with a world of romance that he knew deep down he'd
probably never enter. It was the vicarious thrill, like reading
passionate paperbacks or looking in, through gossip colum-
nists, on the affairs of the stars.

He kept asking himself why he'd even *read* the announcement. Ignorance was, indeed, sometimes bliss, and
this surely was one of those times. If he hadn't known about
Laura's engagement he would have proceeded slowly, on
schedule, meticulously. But now he had to move quickly,
before she got even closer to this lawyer, this former
prosecutor, this intruder. He knew what his first step had to
be. It was the same step he'd taken with each of his victims,

the extension of the apartment-ad link that Karlov would never be able to trace.

* * *

The workday dragged incredibly for Gordon, but as soon as it was over he rushed home. He extracted the needed information from his computer and wrote it carefully in a little notebook.

Then he got into the red Ford.

He drove to a department store that was always open late. The store played a critical role in his crimes, for inside its walls was his favorite phone booth.

It wasn't just any phone booth. It was old, overlooked, and didn't have the soundproofing of modern booths. So there was a metallic echo that slightly disguised Gordon's voice. It was ideal.

Gordon entered the booth and turned inward, magnifying the echo and hiding his face from the crowd in the store. He had an irrational fear of lip-readers, as if there were one in the ladies' sportswear department right outside the booth.

He took a palm-sized Panasonic tape recorder from his pocket and placed its tiny microphone between his ear and the receiver so he could record the call. Then he dropped a quarter into the phone and dialed Laura's number. He heard her phone ring once, then twice, and prayed she'd be in.

"Hello?"

She was.

"Uh, ma'am," Gordon began, slurring his words slightly and sounding rushed, "this is Zenith service, ma'am."

"Oh, I don't have anything broken."

"Uh, no ma'am, that's not why I'm calling. This is a safety recall. You have one of our television receivers."

"Yes, that's right. How did you know?"

"Warranty card supplied by the dealer, ma'am. You've got our model three, with Space Command, serial number 37593A86."

"Well, if you say so."

"I'd appreciate your checking that, ma'am, just to verify. Oh, I am speaking with a Miss Barnett, right?"

"Yes, was that on the card?"

"Yes, ma'am."

"What kind of problem is this, by the way?"

"Oh, well there might be something in the set that requires repair or replacement. We'd only know if we saw it, ma'am."

"I see. Well, let me check that number. What was it?"

"37593A86."

"Just a second."

Gordon could hear Laura putting down the phone and walking across her kitchen floor.

It *always* worked.

In a way, Laura was amused. Glen had bought her the set and she thought it touching that he'd put the warranty in her name. It was a sign of the times. Men had usually regarded technical equipment as entirely their domain.

She looked for the number on the back of the set. It was there, punched into a silver plate. She returned to the phone.

"Hello."

"Yes, ma'am.

"That number's right. Is this very serious, by the way?"

"Potentially, Miss Barnett. There's a transformer that may leak radiation after a certain number of hours."

"Oh . . . *radiation*."

"Believe me, ma'am, there's no danger yet. Your set isn't old enough. But better be safe."

"Of course. You're right. Look, I'm not home during the day."

"I understand. We're doing this after hours."

"Great. When?"

"Next Monday, about eight?"

"Let me check my schedule. Hmm, Monday doesn't look good."

"Okay, Tuesday."

"That's better. I'll write it in for Tuesday. Can we make it earlier, like seven?"

"That's good, ma'am."

"You have my address?"

"It's on the warranty card. Oh, ma'am?"

"Yes?"

"You know that black cover on the back of your set?"

"Well, I've never noticed, but I'll take your word for it."

"Do *not,* ma'am, remove it or tamper with it under any circumstances."

"Oh, I wouldn't think of it."

"Okay, ma'am. We're all set up. If the set needs any adjustments, I can do it then."

"Thanks. See you."

The conversation ended. Gordon turned around in time to confront the glaring face of a woman who'd been waiting for the booth. He smiled at her, and swung open the door. "Sorry."

"The help always get to these phones first," she huffed, and brushed past him into the booth.

"I'll see you in Ladies' Underwear," Gordon mumbled to himself.

He pulled it off, and Laura had fallen for the line. But now he thought of something else: What if that lawyer were there? That would frustrate everything, would turn an evening of ecstasy into bitterness and disappointment.

And yet, maybe he was worrying needlessly. Hadn't Laura changed the date and the hour? Why?

Of course, Gordon reasoned, it was obvious. She'd changed the appointment so it wouldn't conflict with her time with Glen. That's the way a newly engaged woman acted—saving every moment for her intended.

He drove home, confident that he'd thought everything through. Sure, there was still the *chance* that Glen would be there, but the odds were clearly against it.

31

Two days went by and Gordon's mind and body were focused on one woman.

Now he had four days to Tuesday. Four days to Laura.

And now he began the rituals he'd carried out before visiting each victim—rituals he planned with the same care that went into the thrusting of the weapon itself. He had to look different enough from the man who'd inspected Laura's apartment, the fictional Fred Masters, and yet he had to look natural. Most important, he had to strike the image of a repairman, a trained technician, someone who spent his days peering into transistors and tubes. He had practiced the technique repeatedly.

As always, the first step was buying new glasses. Gordon always paid cash and always gave a false name. And he obtained slightly different prescriptions from different optometrists. He got to know the eye-examination procedure so well that he could vary the prescription by the way he answered the examiner's questions. It was a fetish. Never use the same prescription twice. Let there be no record of identical prescriptions being filled around the city in a short period of time. They were all, however, mild prescriptions. He had to see these women. He couldn't afford headaches or dizziness.

He took a bus to East Fifty-ninth Street during a long lunch hour, then walked to an eyeglass store he hadn't patronized before. As always, he picked one in a busy neighborhood, looking for the security of the crowd. He first checked the window, making sure they had what he wanted. Then he walked inside, bucking a group of out-of-town shoppers who'd just ravaged Bloomingdale's about a block away.

"Help you?" someone asked.

The someone was a salesman wearing a phony white smock, giving the impression that he was some kind of Louis Pasteur. He naturally wore glasses. It seemed to be a rule at this shop that all the salespeople wore glasses, whether they needed them or not.

"I've got a prescription," Gordon told him.

"New one?"

"Yeah."

"You sure it's right? We could reexamine you—we've got a special this week..."

"It's right. It's my prescription."

"All right, sir. You want frames. If you buy one pair, you get the second pair at half price, until Tuesday."

"I'll think about it," Gordon said. He'd be happy to come back Wednesday and pay full price, he thought, with Laura Barnett making the selection.

"What did you have in mind?" the salesman asked, looking around Gordon to count the other customers streaming in.

"Something simple. No horn rims, and I don't like those glases without frames on the bottom. Oh, I also don't like those narrow glasses, where you look like you're squinting."

Gordon had visited a number of television repair shops and talked to their technicians, just to get an idea of the kind of glasses technicians wore. They generally wore the standard, roundish, basic, no frills glasses, and a few older ones wore bifocals.

The salesman reached down to a case and pulled out a tray of frames, "all prices," he sniffed, and walked off to another customer, leaving Gordon to make his own selection.

Gordon didn't mind being left alone. It gave him time to try on each frame, to pick the one that would give him the perfect look. Finally, he selected a simple one that made his face look slightly wider. It may have been simple, but it bore the name of one of those nonexistent European designers, and the tag said ninety dollars, and it wasn't on sale. Gordon didn't mind. This was for Laura, the most important woman he'd ever visit, and he was willing to splurge.

The salesman returned, delighted that Gordon was spending so much.

"I'd like the tinted glass," Gordon said. "Green."

"Green?"

"Green."

"Are these sunglasses?"

"No. I want a light tint."

"Sir, most tint, except sunglasses, is in the gray or brown family. Green . . . I don't know."

"I kind of like it," Gordon said. "It's my color." Actually, he realized green was pedestrian, but it was the kind of thing an out-of-fashion repairman might choose.

"Green it is," the salesman said. "Do you want the scratch-proof finish?"

"No."

"It's ten bucks."

"I don't wear glasses that long," Gordon replied. He usually wore them once.

The salesman shrugged and completed Gordon's order. "Tomorrow," he said.

*   *   *

Gordon left the store. His next stop was a shoe shop across town that specialized in special fittings and unusual needs, most of them medically related. When Gordon walked in he saw the usual assortment of customers complaining about walking problems, back problems, leg problems, wife problems, husband problems and doctor bills. The salesmen in this store were trained to be sympathetic, even fawning, because the prices were outrageous and fawning made customers more willing to pay them.

What Gordon wanted was a pair of elevator shoes. This presented a problem because he wasn't short, and it was unusual for someone of normal height to want the item. So he had his story all ready.

"What can I do for you?" asked the smiling salesman, who had some kind of measuring tool in his handkerchief pocket, giving him a bit of a high-tech look. He gazed intently into Gordon's eyes, something else the training program taught, and assumed a concerned expression that had been practiced in company mirrors.

Gordon leaned closer to him. "Uh, this may seem funny..."

"Nothing is funny here, sir," the saleman replied, almost in a whisper, respecting Gordon's obvious wish for privacy. "Your problems are our problems."

"Elevators."

The salesman looked Gordon up and down. "For yourself?"

"Yes. Uh . . . there's this girl."

"Tall," the salesman said.

"You got it."

"We have this all the time. They're getting taller."

"I know. It kills me."

The salesman sat Gordon down in one of the leather-upholstered "rest positions." He took Gordon's size, then started writing notes on a "patient record," just a fancy four-by-six card with the store name on top. "Uh, about how much size did you want?" he asked.

"Inch and a half. I don't want her to notice too much."

"We can serve you. Any style in mind?"

"Black. Plain. I'm your basic guy."

"Yes, sir."

Gordon tried on three or four pairs. He knew never to take the first offering in a specialty house because the easy customer attracts attention. Nor was he intimidated by the pseudomedical atmosphere of this establishment. New York had become boutique city and everything was an act. He was sure the salesmen spent their off-hours telling war stories about the nuts who came into the place, especially the ones who were there to enhance their looks.

Finally, Gordon chose a pair of basic black. But he declined the salesman's recommendation to buy special polish for the imported leather. He wouldn't polish these shoes. In fact, he intended to scuff them up and bend the fronts, making them look like they'd been worn by a man kneeling in back of TVs.

Pity. They were such nice shoes. But they only had to last a night.

*   *   *

Three days to Laura.

Gordon cruised by her apartment house, familiarizing himself again with the neighborhood. He checked the no-parking zones, the meters, the streets marked "patrolled by private guard." He even stopped to check posters on a neighborhood bulletin board. It was summer and sometimes there were night events. If there were anything scheduled for Tuesday night, he wanted to know.

It was Saturday and the neighborhood was jammed, so he wore dark glasses that concealed a good part of his face. He'd hoped to get a glimpse of Laura walking on the sidewalk, but she didn't show.

She was with that lawyer, he assumed.

Then, as he was driving down Central Park West, three blocks from Laura's building, he saw a face he didn't want to see.

Karlov—behind the wheel of his own car, coming from the opposite direction.

Gordon turned away as Karlov passed, baffled as to why the detective would be taking a leisurely cruise through the area. He'd glimpsed Karlov writing something as he drove. But why? Baffled or not, Gordon decided to leave. Staying was not a prudent risk, even though he'd wanted to check the locations of all-night stores and restaurants. He always made it a point not to park near them when he struck. There was too much chance of being noticed.

He drove back to Queens, content that he'd done all he could to prepare for his visit. A haircut and the quick purchase of a new tool kit completed the plan. His advance horoscope for Tuesday said it would be a good day for romance. He didn't believe in horoscopes, but he cut this one out of the paper.

He had the funniest feeling about Laura—that this would be the one who wouldn't resist, that this would be the breakthrough. He had just one regret. He'd have to keep his terrible secret from her the rest of his life. It was a burden he'd have to bear, for he knew he'd never get caught.

*   *   *

Sunday. Two nights to the moment when Gordon West and Laura Barnett would meet again. Laura was with Glen, at her apartment, helping him prepare for his Monday night trip to Cleveland to attend a lawyers' convention. He called it a meeting of thieves called to discuss law and order. The chief justice of the United States would be there, and give a speech, which meant that Glen would have at least a couple of hours to see the sights of Cleveland. He was going only because his firm wanted to be represented. It was a matter of institutional prestige, which sometimes translated into large dollars.

He had most of his clothes carelessly arranged in two suitcases. Laura was an expert packer, Glen the worst. No matter how well she taught him, he couldn't learn the fine art of packing a suit.

"Don't you have an iron?" she asked him, looking through the rubble of his semi-packed belongings.

"An iron?"

"You know. Hot on the bottom, a handle on top."

"Yes, I've seen them. I think my mother had one. I think she even used it once."

"So you're saying you don't have a traveling iron."

"I don't even have one that stays home."

"I'll lend you mine. It's a new Sunbeam. Very good."

"What do I need one for? The hotel has a laundry."

"You want to depend on that?"

"Always have."

"Look, take a traveling iron. Those hotel laundries can

massacre a suit. And it might not be ready on time. Or you might just want to touch things up.''

"Three years of law school, and I'm a laundress," Glen said.

"Don't sweat it. I'll be sitting here listening to records, thinking of you doing your shirts in Cleveland.''

"You do that.''

But then Glen turned serious. The killer was still out there, still prowling this neighborhood, still a threat even to women who'd been meticulously warned. "Look, I want you to be careful," he said. "Do *not* show the apartment.''

"Believe me, I won't.''

"You get a hot prospect, tell him you've got meetings. Arrange the showing for next weekend.''

"I will.''

"People at the office know I'll be away. I've asked Ben Meecham . . . you know Ben . . .''

"Sure. Tall, stooped.''

"Right. I've asked him to call you a few times. It might be late at night. Ben works crazy hours.''

"Look, I'm not a child . . .''

"I know, but I worry. Anything look suspicious, you call Karlov at the Twentieth Precinct. If he's not there, talk to another detective. Call Beer. Use my name. I'll call you every night.''

"Well, I *do* feel protected.''

"Don't feel so protected," Glen warned. "Remember what Karlov said. Feeling it can't happen to you leads to trouble. Think that it *can* happen to you—for your own safety.''

But somehow Laura once again resisted the notion that anything would *actually* happen. In a way, she was glad that Glen was going on this trip. It would give her a chance to reassert her own independence, to show once again that she could survive on her own, as she'd done for years. She was on guard, savvy about the city. She'd be all right.

They finished packing and walked over to the Museum of Natural History, which was having an exhibit on evolution. Glen thought the exhibit would be useful, for one of the subjects at the Cleveland meeting would be the legal challenge to the teachings of evolution in some states.

Evening fell. They went out to dinner. Laura didn't tell Glen about the Zenith repair. It wasn't important. The repairman had her serial number, and that was as good as a fingerprint.

*   *   *

Monday.

As Gordon West dreamed of the rendezvous little more than twenty-four hours away, Leonard Karlov sat in his office with Harold Kramer, who'd just done an autopsy on a young woman murdered with a single knife thrust to the chest. Kramer told Karlov he was sure the murderer hadn't been the serial killer. The victim was married, there were signs of a violent argument, and she'd recently filed for divorce. Suspicions now focused on a boyfriend whom she'd just left and on her husband, who'd save a fortune by killing her.

"The guy tried to make it look like Mr. Serial," Kramer reported. "But it was botched. A pure amateur performance."

"The papers'll grab it, though," Karlov cautioned. "They'll twist it around. They always do."

"Yeah. Probably. By the way, what about your policewomen?" Kramer asked.

"They're doing the job. I'm adding more and removing some of the first ones. We've got a lot of ads out there, but so far no one suspicious has turned up. The guy might not even show, with all the publicity about the real-estate thing. I also did some traveling of my own.''

''Where'd you go?''

''Just the West Side.'' He held up a raft of notes. ''Detective's instinct. With all the killings in the same area, the guy might just like the place. I cruised there Saturday and Sunday, and took the license numbers of all red Fords and Ford-type cars.''

''How many you get?''

''A hundred and six.''

''Jesus.''

''People like red cars. I turned the list over to Motor Vehicles for a license check. I think it's fifty-to-one against finding anything, but it's part of the game.'' He laughed with bitter irony. ''Game. I called it a game.''

''But what can you find? They'll come up with a bunch of names.''

''Then the process begins all over again,'' Karlov said. ''Murder is paperwork, Hal. Always has been, always will be. Each name would have to be checked. I'll answer your next question in advance: yes, it would take weeks or months. But if that guy were driving around over the weekend . . .''

32

Tuesday.

The day.

It was the start of a new heat wave in New York, with temperatures expected to climb into the nineties by midday. Consolidated Edison warned citizens to restrict their use of air conditioners, lest the electrical circuits become overloaded. Older people were warned about the heat. The police were allowing fire hydrants to be opened on some blocks so the local kids could cool off and stay cool, two entirely different concepts. There was a rumor in the air that George Steinbrenner was looking to sell the Yankees, but no one was taking it seriously. There was another rumor that millions were missing from the city treasury, and everyone was taking it seriously.

Gordon West awakened at five A.M., an hour and a half early. He didn't want to awaken. He knew the importance of sleep on a day like this, but he just couldn't relax. So he got up and immediately wondered whether Laura was sleeping alone. He *knew* what the answer was, or thought he did, and it frustrated him. He went immediately to his computer and started reviewing everything he knew about her, making sure he'd committed it to memory. Then he played back the tapes of his phone conversations with her—when he made the appointment to see her apartment, and when he called as a Zenith repairman. He felt close to her.

He checked everything he'd need that night—the glasses, the comb, the elevator shoes, the new lightweight suit, cheap enough for repair work, the tool kit and . . . a new gift for Laura. It was a gold locket with his picture in it. He'd also carry two sharpened screwdrivers in different pockets, and a little can of stain remover, in case things went badly and he got splattered with blood.

He was at work promptly at 8:30, and immediately found a little red slip on his desk summoning him to the grand office of Seymour Merson, boss. He rushed right in, wanting to appear the precise, undistracted employee he'd always been. "You called, Sy?" he asked, gently knocking of Merson's open door.

"Gordon, yes I did," Merson answered, seated behind his desk in an elegant black suit. "Come in, sit down."

Gordon sat, wondering what crisis in classified ads brought him to the boss's desk this early in the morning. "Something wrong?" he asked.

"Good Lord, yes."

"In *our* department?"

"In our department, Gordon. You know all this publicity about that nut out there, the one who murders women?"

"Sure."

"And there's this business that he might be answering our ads?"

"Yeah."

"I'm concerned about it. Our apartment advertising is down four percent this week. I'm worried sick. This guy can hurt our performance graph."

"That's a heartbreaker," Gordon said.

"And that's where *you* come in. Gordon, you're my best man. That's why I let you handle Karlov."

"Thank you, Sy."

"Have the other ad takers *assure* callers that advertising real estate is perfectly safe. All women have to do is take the normal precautions they'd take anyway. We've got to fight back against this guy, Gordon."

"I couldn't agree more," Gordon said. "We ought to contact the realtors and have them run full-page ads on how safe an apartment can be."

"Excellent idea. Do that, too."

"Happy to."

So Gordon West returned to his cubicle, newly charged with the responsibility of rebuilding classified's tarnished image. He felt fully qualified for the task. He had a deep understanding of the problem.

*　　*　　*

Laura was also facing a challenge. The watch company for which she worked had been sold to a cereal manufacturer, and this was the day she was supposed to meet the new "management circle," a psychologist's name for the young hotshot bosses who knew nothing about watches but a lot about oatmeal. Laura was at her desk at nine, wearing her finest summer suit, yet still feeling she was less than acceptable. The heat of an un–air-conditioned bus had had its effect.

At 9:30 she walked into the firm's main meeting room, wearing the proper smile, to meet the new executives. She was told that the meeting had been cancelled. There'd been a late crisis in oatmeal.

The rest of her day was equally dull. There was some concern around the office about staff changes the new management might bring, but no one seriously expected an upheaval soon. She went to lunch with a friend at one. In six hours she would meet the repairman. She made a mental note to tell him about an occasional flicker on her TV screen. He'd probably know what to do.

*   *   *

Midafternoon.

Leonard Karlov got a flash from the police wire. A man in Washington, D.C., had just confessed that *he* was the serial killer wanted in New York. He'd been arrested just outside the National Air and Space Museum, waving a butcher knife at some tourists. The D.C. police, as eager as Brooklyn for a little good publicity, immediately announced the "confession" to the public. Karlov took it seriously because he had to, because all admissions of guilt are taken seriously unless proved false.

Within an hour the subject in Washington had recanted, and it turned out he was just high on drugs. But again, Karlov was hit by reporters' questions and the reminders that the real murderer was still on the loose. He didn't need the reminders. They were all around him, in the victims' files, the reports of other detectives, the newspaper editorials and even a letter from one victim's distant uncle threatening to sue the New York Police Department for gross negligence.

The Department of Motor Vehicles called to say they'd compiled the list of names to go with the license numbers Karlov had collected. Three of the cars turned out to be stolen, so the names of the owners were irrelevant. The cars wouldn't have been in the owners' hands during the murders. The department was ready to mail the list—Parcel Post—when Karlov gently suggested it be sent over by messenger. He couldn't believe the attitude. He just couldn't believe it.

The list arrived within thirty minutes. Karlov hardly looked at it. Instead, he assigned an assistant to make a copy and track down every name, checking for criminal records. It was all part of the tedious effort that would, he'd always told his students, turn up some inconsistency, some piece of information, some scrap of evidence leading to the killer.

It was 4:30 when Sheila McBride appeared at Karlov's door. He hadn't expected her. As director of the project that put policewomen out to lure the killer, she'd been reporting to him by memo, in her usual efficient manner. Karlov had a report on the activities of each policewoman, hour by hour, and the name and background of each man who'd answered their ads.

McBride's eyes flashed urgency. Karlov knew she wouldn't waste his time with trivia, that she had something important, that it couldn't wait. He knew her well. She was the bull's-eye type.

"Come in, Sheila."

McBride strode in rapidly, her red hair even redder than usual in an afternoon sun that barely made it through Karlov's grimy window.

"What happened?" he asked. The thought hit him that a policewoman might have been killed.

"New reports," she said.

"Some strange guy turn up?"

"Maybe."

"Shoot."

"None of my women report anything odd about the

men answering their ads. Regular guys. Legitimate. That's how it seems.''

"Right.''

"But listen to this. Four women got the same ad-taker at the *Register*. We know he's the same from the tapes of the calls.''

"What about him?''

"Chummy.''

"Chummy?''

"Much too chummy. Not just compared to the rest. Compared to anyone in a job like that. It was the questions he asked.''

"Like?''

"Like this. He'd help write the ad. He'd say, 'You enjoy living alone?' He'd get an answer. Then he'd say something like 'You're young and single—direct it toward people like you.' Then he'd wait for their reaction to see if they were both young and single. That kind of thing.''

"Other examples?''

"He warned all of them about the serial killer—but he made sure to ask if they had a doorman at their building.''

Karlov began stirring in his chair. He could easily have dismissed McBride's report as speculation. After all, a friendly ad-taker wasn't scandalous, and warning women about the serial killer wasn't bad. But he started thinking the way *she* was thinking. "More,'' he insisted.

"He was the only ad-taker to ask if they were usually home nights. He said it was important to know the hours the place could be shown. But no one else asked about nights. The others might have asked, 'Any restrictions?' ''

"Sheila,'' Karlov asked, "do you think . . . ?''

"I don't know.''

"One of the key questions is how this killer knows in advance that these women are young and single. Now you bring me someone who not only can answer apartment ads, he *takes* them. He talks to these women, but they never see him. He could answer his own ads, and he would already know he's got young, single women.''

Sheila McBride smiled, one of the few times Karlov had seen her smile. It was the smile of discovery, of breakthrough.

''Who?'' Karlov asked.

McBride took a deep breath. She knew Karlov's entire operation. She'd visited the paper, talked with the people in classified aids. ''Gordon West,'' she replied.

33

An air-conditioning failure closed Laura's company early. She thought she might do some shopping, but the heat was impossible and she took a bus directly home.

Once inside her building she went to the little room on the lobby floor where the mail boxes were lined up row by row. She saw through the little window of her mailbox that she had mail. She opened the box and pulled out a handful of envelopes, inevitable bills and the just-as-inevitable ads for carpet cleaning, floor polishing and bargain-priced legal services ("uncontested divorce—$200"). She started flipping through them.

She expected the bill from Bloomingdale's and the price quotes from Mr. Windemere, the photographer. She wasn't interested in the uncontested divorces, so she flipped that mailer into a nearby trash can.

But then she came to something curious—a business-size white envelope with no return address, and her name and address printed in neat, red ballpoint pen. She didn't get things like this. She looked at the postmark and saw that it came from New York. Almost instantly, a thought raced through her mind: it was another of those chain letters, those anonymous messages that tell the recipient to send it on to four others, or risk a spell of the worst kind of luck.

Sure. That's what it was.

She hated them, and she resented the people who sent them. It was an imposition, an act of arrogance, an invasion of her privacy. Still, she opened the envelope.

There was no chain letter inside. Instead she found a plain greeting card with a rose printed on it. Scrawled in that same red ballpoint ink was, *You will be mine. Now and forever.* And also inside the envelope were scores of little letters of the alphabet, all cut neatly from newspaper headlines.

Who?

Who could have sent this bizarre package?

It couldn't have been Jason, for this wasn't his handwriting and wasn't the kind of thing Jason would do. And it sure wasn't Glen, who prided himself on impeccable penmanship and who would never try to frighten her. Maybe it was the same guy who'd sent those anonymous gifts—and maybe he was some admirer who didn't want to come forward.

And what were those letters doing there? What did they mean, all cut up like that and lying in the envelope? Did they spell out something, or were they some kind of practical joke? Instantly, Laura thought of calling Karlov, but almost as instantly she rejected the notion. This might just be a prank, someone's idea of a great stunt. How foolish she'd feel if the police put those letters together and they spelled out something like *Congratulations* or *Happy Engagement* or something similar. Maybe *she* should try to put them together, to figure out the puzzle, if there was one.

She took the elevator upstairs, still clutching the batch of mail in her hands, the mystery card on top. She went to her apartment and immediately flipped on the air conditioner. Then Laura sat down at the kitchen table, emptied the envelope of letters and tried to make sense of the little slips of paper.

She'd never been very good at crossword puzzles, and usually avoided the challenging one in the *New York Times*. Nor had she been the greatest Scrabble player. A slight breeze from the air conditioner swept a few of the letters off the table, further complicating her work.

She didn't get very far. No combination that she put together seemed to lead anywhere, and she soon realized that this was a mystery she wasn't going to solve.

34

Karlov was utterly thrown.

"West? *West?* I know West. He's..."

"...been helping us," McBride said.

"I can't believe it," Karlov snapped, using words that he knew no detective should use. "Gordon West? Now look, this is only a theory. I mean, West *is* very efficient and very helpful. Your women could be imagining things."

"Could be," McBride agreed. "But it wasn't the helpfulness. It was the questions. Specific questions."

Karlov couldn't counter that. Gordon West had gotten those women to let down their guard. He'd asked them questions that in other circumstances they might have found offensive. Yet he had this knack of making them think he was just doing his job.

But it couldn't be, could it? Would a killer operate with such nerve, even when he knew the police were closing in?

Karlov had to play devil's advocate. "Look," he asked McBride, "is it possible he *was* just trying to be helpful, that he got the idea for these questions from all the publicity over the killer? Maybe he's just sensitive to the dangers facing single women."

"That's always possible," McBride agreed. "But when four women detect the same thing . . ."

"Granted." And Karlov knew that being an ad-taker gave a killer a marvelous opportunity to prescreen his victims. "What if it *is* West?" he asked. "How does he operate? We know that most of the past victims never showed apartments at night. Some of them weren't even living in the places they advertised when they were killed."

"Maybe he kept in touch with them," McBride said.

"Maybe. He could've developed personal relationships."

Without another word, Karlov went to his phone. He dialed the number for the paper and asked for Seymour Merson. Then he cupped his hand over the receiver. "I have only one question," he told McBride. "I hope I can trust this guy. I couldn't the last time."

"Merson," came the voice at the other end, official and earth-shaking as always.

"Mr. Merson, this is Detective Karlov."

"Of course."

"I need a piece of information. I'm going to ask that you keep this entirely confidential. You're the only one who knows, so any leak is easily traced."

"I understand. You *can* trust me," Merson said, embarrassed that he'd released the real-estate connection.

"Do you have Gordon West's personnel folder?"

"Yes, in my cabinet. Why?"

"Just checking, for background. Could you tell me his home town?"

"I'll get that for you. Is Gordon in some kind of trouble?"

"Oh, not at all. This is for a special purpose, possibly a commendation."

"I see." Merson was disappointed. Why wasn't *he* getting one. But he left his desk, went to the file and brought back a folder. He opened it to the first page and ran his finger down the data. "Uh, Detective?"

"Yes."

"Gordon comes from . . . Winnetka, Illinois."

There was a long silence. "Winnetka," Karlov finally whispered. "Tell me, did he go to high school there?"

"High school? Let me find that. Yes, yes he went to high school in Winnetka. Class of sixty-four."

"Yes," Karlov replied, as the focus started getting sharper and sharper. "The class of sixty-four. Thank you. Thank you very much. Mr. Merson, do *not* discuss this call with him. I must emphasize that. It could be a felony."

"A felony? For a commendation?"

"I can't go into details. But this will *not* leave your office."

"No, no, of course not. Absolute silence. I personally guarantee it." Now Merson was thoroughly intimidated. The phone call wouldn't leave his office. He didn't need that kind of trouble. He didn't want to blow the chance for *his* commendation.

*　　*　　*

Karlov hung up. "Winnetka," he sighed. "Winnetka, Illinois, class of sixty-four." He flipped a pencil at a wall, then just stared off into space. The old questions were coming back to haunt him. What had he missed, what subtle clue had he overlooked, what item had he misplaced, that allowed him to work with Gordon West, to talk with him, to look into his eyes, yet never know? "Sheila," he said, "you gave us this break. You deserve the credit."

"It wasn't me," McBride countered. "You set up the policewoman network. It was a dragnet. It did what it was supposed to do."

Even in this deflated moment, Karlov knew that McBride was right, and some of his pride was salvaged.

It took him only a few seconds to zip through the car-registration list from the Department of Motor Vehicles, compiled from the plate numbers he'd taken down over the weekend. He quickly spotted the computer-generated entry, WEST, G., and license number 4309BLN. He spun the list around toward McBride and pointed to the name. He realized that he'd passed West's car and never noticed the driver. And he might never have guessed from looking at this list that WEST, G., was Gordon West. West was such a common last name.

"Resentment," Karlov said. "This whole case revolves around resentment."

"How do you figure that?"

"That lady in Great Neck, Deborah Stone, gave me pictures from her graduating class—prom pictures, some other ones, too. Gordon West wasn't in those pictures. I would have remembered him, remembered his face, certainly remembered his name. All those pictures had *full* names. He was probably a social misfit, the kind who didn't show up because he just didn't make it. And I'll bet it was West who stole those gondolas after the sixty-four prom—out of spite, out of resentment, to get back at those who kept him out."

"A rejected boy," McBride said.

"Yes, and rejected even today. Sheila, he killed these women in New York because—I'm giving a theory—they also rejected him in some way."

"Why did he keep those gondolas and put them at the victims' heads?" McBride asked.

"They're symbols. I've seen this in murder before. It's a kind of bravado. 'Here, look at me, Winnetka,' he's saying. 'I made it. I'm on the map!' It's all in his mind, of course."

"And it all fits."

* * *

They left the office. Karlov arranged for a search warrant so he could go through West's apartment if he had to, then he and McBride got into his car and raced to the paper to make the arrest. It was a moment of triumph, yet not complete triumph. Karlov knew that all the evidence against West was circumstantial. West had asked personal questions of advertisers. He had driven his car through the area of the murders. He had gone to high school in Winnetka and graduated in 1964. He appeared in no high school pictures and might have been a social reject. But Karlov had not actually placed West at the scene of any of the crimes. Instinct, though, told him West was the kind to confess under intense questioning—the type whose ego would push him to more bravado, to boasting of the crimes. Even if he didn't confess, Karlov was sure there'd be incriminating evidence in his apartment.

When he arrived at the paper he and McBride rushed to the classified advertising section. Karlov's heart pounded. No matter how many arrests he'd made, each one was high drama, this one the highest of all.

Gordon wasn't in his cubicle.

Karlov went to Seymour Merson's office. "Where's West?" he asked Merson.

"Why?"

"I've got to talk to him."

"About the commendation?"

"And other things."

"He's gone home. Said he didn't feel too well."

"What was bothering him?"

"He just said he had a headache and pains. The usual cold."

"Thanks," Karlov said.

"I'd be happy to help," Merson volunteered, a broad, overly gracious smile on his face. The thought of a police commendation for him danced before his eyes.

"I appreciate that," Karlov replied. "I'll be calling on you. It'll be important."

"I'll be here."

Karlov returned to his car with McBride. He radioed ahead for other detectives to join him at West's apartment house in Queens. Surprising a man at work was easy. Rapping on his door at home might provoke resistance, even a quick destruction of evidence before the door was opened. Karlov wanted to take West alive. He wanted to question him, probe his mind, find out what he was really like. And Leonard Karlov, as human as any officer, looked forward to standing with his suspect before the cameras and microphones, receiving the adulation of the city, vindicated after his struggle to solve the serial murders.

He and McBride crossed the Fifty-ninth Street Bridge and drove up Queens Boulevard. This was enemy country.

"What if he has an alibi for even *one* of the murder nights?" McBride asked.

Karlov didn't answer. This wasn't the moment for nightmares.

35

It was 5:45 P.M. and Gordon West couldn't wait. In one hour and fifteen minutes he would have Laura alone.

VICTORY, he tapped into his computer, next to her name. It was premature, but it felt good. He'd never used that word before.

He knew that Laura would never put all those letters together in the right order, would never realize that they spelled out the names of all his previous victims. He chuckled at his little joke, his little act of daring. He wished he could bring it up to her when they met again, to prove his wit and intelligence.

He shaved quickly, brushed his hair back in a different style, and put on his new glasses, elevator shoes and suit. To change his appearance even more, he used touches of stage makeup, shading his skin and narrowing his eyes. He grabbed his tool kit. He was out by 6:06.

He entered his car and drove off just as Leonard Karlov pulled up to the building's front door. The two never saw each other.

Other detectives arrived. Karlov, McBride and two men rode up in the elevator. They rushed to West's door and went through the ritual, first knocking sharply.

"Open up, police!"

No answer.

Karlov knocked again.

Again no answer. A man had been assigned to find the superintendent, who quickly arrived with a master key. Under authority of his search warrant, Karlov had the door opened and entered the apartment.

It was dark, the shades drawn, the lights out, yet everything was neat and in place. It was the apartment of any meticulous man. Nothing was very unusual except the extreme darkness. A few years earlier, Karlov would have thought the home computer odd, but they were becoming consumer items, common and unexceptional.

But where was West?

He'd left work, he'd said, because he was sick. "Maybe he's at the doctor," McBride guessed.

"Or maybe he had to pick up some things, maybe medicine," Karlov added.

But Merson hadn't described West as very sick. The illness, if there was one, sounded mild. Most men would come right home and stay there. Karlov didn't like the setup. He didn't feel like waiting around for Gordon West— he knew what Gordon West might be doing.

"I hope this isn't one of his nights," he told McBride. Then he contemplated the computer. "He uses one of those at work, doesn't he?"

"Sure. All the ad-takers do," McBride answered.

"So why does he have one here? His life isn't complicated."

"Hobby maybe."

Karlov rapidly went through West's drawers. He was struck by the lack of records. "No files, no notes, no nothing," he said. Again, he looked at that computer. "I'll bet his whole life is in there."

But *there* was a barrier. Karlov couldn't operate a computer. "Anyone?" he asked.

Sheila McBride stepped up to the keyboard. She'd taken a police course in computer science to be up on the latest technology.

She turned on the machine. The screen lit up in a bright gray hue. There was a little file of floppy disks next to the computer, and McBride put one in, playing it back and skipping around, trying to find anything related to the case. But the first three disks dealt only with home finance and income taxes. Dull stuff. Routine.

The fourth disk was different.

It had names. Familiar names. Names like Constance Rainey and Deborah Moore and Marie Gould, Carol Krindler and Sabrina Brent. Victims' names. And with each name was a file of information neatly arranged in columns of green type on that gray screen: the date of the victim's first call to place an ad; personality characteristics; reason for wanting to move; marital status; type of building; address; description of neighborhood; parking conditions; a detailed description of the apartment and virtually everything in it.

And at the end of each file was the phrase SUBJECT TERMINATED in bold capitals.

Now there was no doubt. Gordon West had killed those women. He'd answered his own apartment ads, and then somehow had gotten back into the apartments at night, or into other apartments the victims had moved to months later.

"Well organized," Karlov remarked as he glanced at the material on the screen.

"I wonder why he needed all of it, though," Sheila McBride said.

"Overkill maybe," Karlov replied. "Maybe he was an information nut, just like some people are news nuts. He liked to have everything he knew about these women on those disks." But Karlov wasn't satisfied with that answer. The disks did seem overloaded with information, much of it trivial and useless. Who really cared about the model number of Deborah Moore's microwave oven?

It was 6:20.

Laura Barnett had forty minutes.

*   *   *

Gordon drove over the Fifty-ninth Street Bridge, heading for Laura's apartment. The drive was swift and easy. Even the heat seemed to be less stifling, allowing him to set the car's air conditioner on low. He rehearsed what he wanted to say to Laura after the repairman business was swept out of the way. This had to be right. Special. No antagonizing her. No quick moves that would panic her or send her running to another room. Gordon West was a man who had learned from experience. He didn't want to have to kill Laura. He was sure he could get her to be reasonable.

"I just think you're attractive," he mumbled, loud enough to hear himself over the blowing of the air conditioner. "I hope you don't mind." That was it. Be courteous, dignified without being humble. "I know you're seeing this lawyer, but nothing in life is forever." No, that wasn't right. That was *too* personal. Maybe she really liked the guy. Maybe she'd have to *see* that there was something better out there, something named Gordon West. No, don't attack the lawyer, just ignore him. Charm Laura. Do it with style.

"I'd like to give you a tour of the paper. You'd like that." Sure she would. Everyone is interested in the workings of a great newspaper. Gordon felt he was perfecting a smooth approach that wouldn't scare Laura, but would make her comfortable and confident. He knew he could do it. He'd just never given himself the chance.

He looked to the right in time to see a patrol car pass. He still felt a tinge of fear when a police car pulled up beside him. He knew that, even if he were stopped for some minor infraction, the policeman could become suspicious and start searching the car, ultimately finding the gondola. But the two policemen looked straight ahead.

Less than a minute later, police radios crackled with an all points bulletin warning of a red 1981 Ford sedan, license 4309BLN. Karlov had ordered an alert for Gordon West's car.

Gordon entered Manhattan, his lips still moving with lines to be delivered to Laura Barnett. A driver coming from the other direction looked right at him. Gordon's lips stopped— his fear of lip-readers.

He crossed Central Park and swung up Central Park West, turning into Laura's block. A police car passed on a cross street, but didn't notice him. In keeping with his rigid plan, he drove two blocks past Laura's building and parked. It was still light, but he parked away from a street lamp so his car would be in the shadows when he returned.

He got out and walked.

It was 6:28.

Thirty-two minutes to Laura. His insides were red hot.

*   *   *

Karlov and McBride shot through disk after disk, desperate for some thread that would lead to Gordon. The disks were packed with data on young, single women.

Then they found Laura's name.

Next to it was the standard information.

But then that one word: VICTORY.

"What does it mean?" he asked McBride.

She shrugged. "Maybe they clicked."

"No, I interviewed her. I'm sure she would've come clean."

"You *really* sure?"

"No," Karlov admitted. "Not a hundred percent."

"Then we're back to your question: what does *victory* mean?"

"I don't know, but this is the only name that has that word. She's attractive, a logical target. And that word."

Karlov flashed through the data on Laura Barnett—the physical description, Glen, her apartment. It struck him that West would make an excellent detective.

Then, suddenly, his narrow face hardened. His eyes seemed to squint, as if seeing something not quite believable.

Wait, this couldn't be. No, it couldn't. Too obvious. Too simple. But maybe . . .

Without saying a word, he went for Gordon's phone and called the Twentieth Precinct.

Sergeant Sheen was on watch.

"Twentieth Precinct, Sergeant Sheen," came the sing-songy automatic voice. "What can I do for you?"

"Sheen, Karlov."

"Sir."

"I want immediate protection for one Laura Barnett. I'll give you her address. Under no circumstances is anyone to enter her apartment. Clear?"

"Yes, sir. Clear."

"Good."

Karlov rattled off Laura's address and Sheen took it down. Then Karlov hung up and turned to McBride. "I've got it," he said. "All these serial numbers, for Laura Barnett's television set, her air conditioner, her refrigerator. One of the victims wrote CALL BACK on a chalkboard. She meant *recall, product recall*. You know, the manufacturer comes and repairs a defect in an appliance. That's the connection. This guy gets these serial numbers and..."

He reached again for the phone.

He tapped out her number.

* * *

Frustrated by the mystery card and the loose letters, Laura went out for some neighborhood shopping, then hurried home for her appointment with the Zenith man.

She entered her apartment at 6:40. The red light was flashing on her answering machine. She was sure Glen had called. The man had gone nuts in the one day he'd been away, calling her three times at the office.

She walked over to the machine and pressed PLAY. The thing started to rewind, with the rapid-fire gibberish of a tape going backward at high speed. Finally it stopped, and began playing back. The first message was from a picture-frame store announcing that the frame Laura had ordered had come in. Then there was a call from a friend simply asking Laura to call back. Then, a third message.

"Uh, Ms. Barnett, this is—"

At that instant the phone rang. Laura snapped off the machine and picked up. It was her mother. They talked. She'd play back the message later. The voice on the tape, in those first words, had sounded familiar, but, since it came through that tinny little speaker, she wasn't able to place it.

"Hi, mom, how're you feeling?"

It was always Laura's first question to her mother, good for an answer lasting up to ten full minutes.

*   *   *

Gordon was approaching Laura's building, which was caught in the deepening shadows of the setting sun. It was 6:58. His heart throbbed wildly. A gondola rested at the bottom of his tool kit. But somehow he was sure he wouldn't need it.

He entered the vestibule and popped a cough drop into his mouth, relaxing his throat, allowing his voice to sound deeper. He covered his fingertip with a tissue and rang Laura's buzzer.

It rang sharply in Laura's kitchen. "Mom, the door. Gotta go." She wrapped up the conversation and flipped on her intercom. "Yes?"

"Zenith, ma'am."

"Okay. Expecting you." Laura pressed her buzzer, unlocking the building's front door.

Now the way was clear for Gordon West.

There were no policemen to stop him—despite Leonard Karlov's urgent request.

Six fifty-nine.

Gordon waited for the elevator to return to the lobby. Then he rode alone to Laura's floor.

Seven P.M.

On time. Always on time. The mark of a meticulous man. Gordon West rang Laura's doorbell, a two-part chime.

Laura was already at the door waiting. She opened. "Hi," she said. "Thanks for being on time." She eyed the clock, knowing Glen would call at eight.

"We try to keep to the schedule, ma'am," Gordon replied as he walked in. He closed the door, discreetly nudging the lock open in case he had to get out fast.

She did think she knew that face, or that voice, or something. But Gordon had done a remarkable makeover, and Laura really believed this was a Zenith repairman. Like the other women Gordon had visited, she couldn't get the connection straight. The name Fred Masters didn't immediately come to mind.

"It's over here," she said, walking toward her TV.

"Okay. This'll only be a few minutes."

"Oh," Laura said, as Gordon put his toolbox next to the set, "sometimes the picture rolls."

"Top to bottom, ma'am, where you see black lines between the frames?"

"Yes."

"It happen often?"

"No, but sometimes when I change stations . . ."

"Probably your vertical hold. There's a little knob in the back. I'll adjust it for you."

"Thanks."

Gordon slipped behind the TV. Go through the motions, he told himself. Be real. Put her at ease. He started unscrewing the back of the set.

Just then Laura remembered the unplayed message on her machine, interrupted when her mother called. Casually, she walked over to the machine, which was in her kitchen. She stood at the kitchen entrance to operate it, in full view of Gordon.

She pressed REWIND to get back to the start of the message, then PLAY.

"Uh, Ms. Barnett, this is Detective Karlov. Listen carefully, ma'am. You're the target of the serial killer. We know who he is."

Laura froze, staring into the machine.

Gordon heard. Clearly. He fought to keep control, his hands remaining on the back of the TV.

But he looked at Laura, his face flashing surprise.

Anyone hearing that message would *have* to look at her. Keep it real. Even now, keep it real!

"Let no one in your apartment," Karlov went on, "even if he knows the serial number of every item you have."

He paused. A mistake, Laura prayed. Let it be a mistake.

"Ms. Barnett, he's posing as a *repairman*."

Laura spun toward Gordon. At that instant, she saw herself dead, sprawled out on her own living-room floor.

And then Karlov described him.

Even Gordon's expert makeover couldn't mask Karlov's details. And finally, as Laura stared into that face, as she heard Karlov's voice, the recognition came. "Masters," she whispered.

Gordon did not answer.

"I'm sending help," Karlov said. Then the machine clicked off.

Silence.

Silence between Laura Barnett and Gordon West.

"You," Laura finally whispered, still too shocked to move.

Gordon West felt an incipient terror. A terror mixed with a strange relief. With remarkable calm he placed his tools on the rug. But he still stared at Laura, who was now standing with her left hand tight against her mouth.

"A repairman," she said, amazed at how she'd been taken.

"I came because I like you," Gordon said. "Don't be afraid of me."

"You were here before."

"Yes. That's when I decided how much I like you. Most of the other women, they never realized I'd visited them. I was just another blur in the apartment-hunting crowd. Only one did. It was too bad. Please don't be afraid."

But Laura started backing up as Gordon began walking slowly toward her. "I sent you those presents," he said. "That shows how much I think of you. There's nothing wrong with sending presents. I'm sure your lawyer friend sends you presents."

"Go away," Laura demanded, now back against the refrigerator, the vibration of its motor buzzing through her.

"I won't hurt you," Gordon said. "I just want to get to know you."

"This is *no* way."

"Okay, but girls never . . . I mean, I'm not the luckiest guy in the world. Understand? They turn me down. This is my *only* way. We could go out . . ."

"No!"

"Oh, yes." He walked closer, the clicking of his footsteps slapping off the kitchen walls. "We'll get to know each other real well."

"Never!"

Suddenly, Gordon's eyes flashed with anger.

He was failing.

He *always* failed.

He knew what he had to do, but hated it.

36

Karlov barreled toward the West Side, Sheila McBride beside him. As he lurched around the corner of Sixty-fifth Street and Central Park West, turning north, he snapped on his radio, calling the Twentieth Precinct. Sergeant Sheen picked up.

"Sheen."

"This is Karlov."

"Sir."

"Give me the status of that crew I requested for Laura Barnett."

"Yes, sir. Hold, sir."

Sheen clicked off his radio, apparently to consult with some other officer. Karlov was annoyed that Sheen didn't have the information at his fingertips. "I wonder what's so important over there," he complained to McBride. "Parking tickets?"

"Probably."

"One big bureaucracy," Karlov mumbled.

Then Karlov's radio clicked as Sheen came back on the line.

"Sir."

"Yes?"

"On that protection for Barnett, Laura..."

"Yes, Sheen, go ahead."

"Not authorized, sir."

"What?"

"No authorization. Captain Maddox, he didn't authorize it. No, sir."

Karlov's face turned beet red. His eyes, often squinty, now bulged with fury. "He didn't authorize... *why?*"

"Uh, sir, he's out right now. But one of the fellas says this Barnett was a chronic complainer. She complained twice about some fellow sending her presents or something ... and none of it turned out important. There was no felony. So the captain said this was probably another complaint, and he said that the men had too much to do. Y'know, we're really goin' after the double parkers this week."

"Did *Captain* Maddox know that *I* requested the protection?" Karlov barked.

"Oh, sure, sir. He said he'd talk to you about it. Or you could call him at home."

"Thank you," Karlov snapped. "And thank the captain. Tell him I'm moved by his courtesy."

"I guess you're angry, sir."

Karlov clicked off the radio and stepped on the gas. Laura was unprotected. *He* was the only thing that stood between her and Gordon West.

"Double parking," he told McBride. "They second-guessed me so they wouldn't have to take anyone off double parking. Brilliant."

* * *

Laura knew what was coming. She'd read the papers. She'd seen the TV reports. She knew that the thrust to the chest was next, and all she could think of was Glen, and what he'd find, and how he'd react, and what he'd do for the rest of his life.

"Don't resist me," Gordon demanded. "Please don't resist me. I don't want to hurt you, but if you resist, I'll have to. It's punishment. That's all. It's right to be punished when you do something wrong. We were all taught that when we were kids, weren't we? You do something wrong, you get punished."

They were three feet apart in the kitchen, their eyes meeting, Laura still not believing what was happening. Gordon blocked one exit from the kitchen, but there was another. Laura didn't eye it. She didn't dare. She didn't dare take her eyes off Gordon.

But, suddenly, she spun around and bolted through the hallway to her bedroom. She flew inside, slammed the door and locked it.

Now her mind began to clear. She had time, maybe only seconds or minutes, but *time*.

The phone.

Get the phone and call the police.

She went for her night table, reaching out for the receiver in a swift, automatic action.

But it wasn't there.

Glen had taken it to the living room Sunday night. Neither of them had put it back.

Laura stared at the empty space on her night table. All she could think of was an empty space in a cemetery, ready for her.

Gordon pounded on the door. The sound reverberated

through the apartment. Laura could see the door panels buckling under Gordon's repeated, passionate blows.

She prayed that someone would hear the noise and bring help.

But what good would it do? She assumed the front door was locked. Gordon would get to her before help came. And screaming wouldn't help at all, would only infuriate him more.

There had to be a way out.

The blows to the door became sharper, metallic.

Gordon wasn't using fists now. He was using a hammer from his tool kit.

Laura's eyes flew around the room. She had to have *something*, some weapon.

Her eyes stopped at her closet, its sliding door open. There was an object on a shelf.

He was sick—a sick man with a fantasy. Play to his fantasy. *Use* it.

Gordon kept hacking away. "I'll punish you!" he shouted. He knew there was no hope she'd see reason. She *was* just like the others—too ready to reject him, like the girls in Winnetka who had rejected him.

Finally, he slammed the center of the door sharply.

The hammer broke through, sending splinters into the bedroom. It would only be seconds.

He prepared to hit the door again, thrusting the hammer back over his head.

But then, incredibly, the door began to open.

Slightly, then more, then more.

Gordon stood in disbelief.

Only one person could be opening it.

Laura.

The door was open. There was Laura, standing. Peaceful, calm.

She stood before Gordon West, holding the object she'd spotted on her closet shelf—the bottle of champagne she'd received anonymously. Now there was no doubt in her mind who'd sent it.

"I gave that to you," Gordon said, almost in a whisper.

"Yes, I know," Laura replied. "Look, why don't we talk things over. A little champagne never hurt."

"Yes," Gordon said, confused and off guard.

"I understand you now," Laura told him. "I didn't understand you before, but now I do. You're really okay. But some of those other women didn't realize it."

These were the words Gordon West always wanted to hear.

"Maybe we can get together," she said, shivering underneath. "My engagement is wrong. I really don't like Glen that much."

"I can understand that," Gordon said.

"I like *strong* men . . . like you."

Gordon was silent. He loved it.

But he lived only partially in a fantasy world. "You don't mean that," he said.

"Why don't we find out?"

That was the key, she thought. Tantalize him. Bewitch him. Then maneuver toward the front door. Rush into the corridor and grab the ax near the fire hose.

"Let's have a drink," she said, "in the living room."

She started walking. Gordon walked a few steps with her, bathing in his fantasy.

Then he stopped. Cold. He spun toward her. Furious. Livid. No, he *wasn't* stupid. In that instant he hated her, loathed her. *She* was the worst of all. The others had only resisted. She'd teased him, demeaned him.

Suddenly, he reached into an inside pocket and took out a sharpened screwdriver.

He trapped Laura against a wall.

But . . . no, he thought. Not the screwdriver. That was pedestrian. Ordinary. He'd done it so many times before.

The champagne. Smash it against the wall. Then use the jagged glass. It would be the perfect vengeance.

He reached for it. But Laura slipped it away, forcing him off balance. He reached again. "Give that to me!" he shouted, his moves frustrated.

Then Laura saw an opening. She swung the bottle at him—and missed.

He charged at her. She swung again.

She hit him squarely in the head.

The bottle exploded like a grenade, sending its shrapnel out in a burst of fury, away from Laura.

Gordon went down.

His cuts were minor, superficial. But he was stunned, shocked, champagne coating his head and face, fogging his eyes.

Even in his confusion, though, he managed to reach up quickly and grab Laura's arm. She tried desperately to pull away.

Then . . . voices. In the hallway. A man and a woman, searching for an apartment.

A rap of the door.

"Police! Open up!"

But the door *was* open. Gordon had left it unlocked for his own quick exit. In a flash it flew open.

Karlov stood there, McBride behind him.

They'd never seen anything like it—a mass killer, stunned by a potential victim, still trying to kill her.

"Freeze!" Karlov ordered, leveling his pistol at Gordon's head.

Gordon could see with one eye now. And he froze. He still grasped Laura's arm. The screwdriver had fallen to the carpet, but he had a second, in another pocket.

One lightning thrust, he knew, and he might kill her before Karlov got off a shot.

But no, he wouldn't do that. Not Gordon West. He would go out with style, with class, the extraordinary man who'd baffled an entire police force for weeks.

No last-minute bloodshed for him.

"It would've been fun," he told Laura, and released her. She stepped away, still holding the jagged top of the champagne bottle. She gazed at the man who would have been her murderer, on his knees, champagne dripping down over his clothing.

"This man took your apartment ad at the paper," Karlov told her.

She was startled, momentarily baffled. Then things became sharper. "He answered his own ad," she said.

"That's right. Then he came here with his little notebook, and recorded the serial numbers of every appliance you own."

Laura turned to West, a cold anger crossing her face. "That's how you got the number of my TV set," she said.

"And of course you didn't question him," Karlov explained. "People are snowed by numbers. If he had the serial number, he had to be legitimate. And that's how he got back in, claiming he was arranging safety recalls of TV sets. That's how he got to kill those other girls."

"How did you know it was me?" Gordon asked, still trying to sound strong.

"Policewomen," Karlov replied. "You've been talking to them every day. You just didn't know when to stop. That was your mistake, West."

Gordon hated that word: mistake. He wasn't supposed to make mistakes. His was the perfect technique, the fool-proof plan. He was *uncatchable*.

"Mistake" sent another word slicing through his confused mind. Humiliation. Again humiliation.

This time, humiliation brought on by policewomen.

He'd be paraded in front of television cameras, handcuffed, for all those people back in Winnetka to see. He wouldn't have his revenge. He wouldn't be able to point another gondola at them, mocking them, accusing them, ridiculing them.

Karlov stepped toward him. The handcuffs came out.

Gordon looked away as Karlov snapped them on, the final click as devastating to Gordon West as the knife thrust he'd perfected on those women.

Karlov started leading him out as Laura watched, still stunned by her brush with death.

*   *   *

Karlov and West passed Sheila McBride. West stopped. "You're nice," he said to McBride.

"Thank you," McBride answered coolly.

"When I get out, I'll look you up. We'd get along. I always get along with the girls."

Karlov led him out.

*   *   *

It wasn't long. It was only a matter of minutes, but to Laura it seemed like hours. The phone finally rang.

"Dull meeting," were Glen's romantic first words.

"I'm sure," Laura replied.

"Totally useless. A lot of trivia. Anything exciting happen there?"

"Of course not," Laura answered.

"What'd you do tonight?"

"Tonight? Oh, I had the TV repaired."

"Anything else?"

"I knocked off that champagne."

"Alone?"

"No . . . with the repairman."

"With the—?"

"I'll explain it when you get home. We'll have time. Years and years of time."

About the Author

An internationally acclaimed novelist, William Katz is the author of six previous books, including the bestseller *Surprise Party*—which the *St. Louis Post-Dispatch* called "an orgy of anguished fright." William Katz was educated at the University of Chicago and Columbia University, and was an editor of the *New York Times Magazine*. He currently resides in Scarsdale, New York.

By the year 2000, 2 out of 3 Americans could be illiterate.

It's true.

Today, 75 million adults… about one American in three, can't read adequately. And by the year 2000, U.S. News & World Report envisions an America with a literacy rate of only 30%.

Before that America comes to be, you can stop it… by joining the fight against illiteracy today.

Call the Coalition for Literacy at toll-free **1-800-228-8813** and volunteer.

Volunteer Against Illiteracy. The only degree you need is a degree of caring.

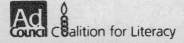

Ad Council Coalition for Literacy

Warner Books is proud to be an active supporter of the Coalition for Literacy.